Say Yes to Everything

(A comical Christmas Romance)

by

Michele E. Northwood

© 2023

Copyright© 2023 by Michele E. Northwood

This book is a work of fiction. Apart from known historical places, all characters, and incidents are the product of the author's imagination and are fictitious. All rights reserved. No part of this book may be reproduced or transmitted in any form or by any means, electronically or mechanically, including photocopying, recording or by any information storage and retrieval system, without the author's permission.

Cover Art by Get Covers.com

Book formatting by Randy V. Perez

An ode to all non-British readers

This poem is to apologise/apologize

I do not wish to offend your eyes,

But I'm a Brit and you may think

My spelling's completely on the blink (fritz).

My sombre/somber poem's for you to see,

You do not write the same as me

You use a `z´ when I use `s´

In cosy/cozy and idealised/idealized - I guess...

I add a `u´ when you do not,

In honour/honor and colour/color (It happens a lot!)

Ambience/ambiance and travelling/traveling

Our difference in spelling is a curious thing!

So as you manoeuvre/maneuver through this book,

And at these differences, you look,

Mistakes for you are not for me.

(It's how I was taught, you see).

I need to emphasise/emphasize this well...

Before you assume I cannot spell!

I hope you'll enjoy this book you've bought.

and not give these differences another thought.

Kind regards,

Michele xx

Chapter One: Get a Job!

Chapter Two: Hi Ho! It's off to work she goes.

Chapter Three: All I want for Christmas is Poo!

Chapter Four: Christmas is Cancelled.

Chapter Five: The Face that Launched a Thousand Hits.

Chapter Six: An unwanted Blind Date.

Chapter Seven: A Television Sensation.

Chapter Eight: Gotcha!

Chapter Nine: Kate Gets her Strop on.

Chapter Ten: Christmas Day.

Chapter Eleven: The Cruise.

'An Education for Emma'. First Chapter and Blurb

About the author

Chapter One.

Get a job!

December 5th

Kate Massey sat in her mother's big armchair, feeling sorry for herself. Her skinny four-foot-eight frame was an easy fit even with her knees drawn up to her chest. Still dressed in her pyjamas at six o'clock in the evening, she clutched a large gin and tonic, sucking the contents up a straw like a little girl. Depressed wasn't a strong enough word for how she felt, living back at her parents' home after all these years.

Nothing much had changed in her absence. The same Christmas tree she remembered as a child stood in the front window. The sparkling lights danced to a different rhythm than the strip lights around the window. She doubted anyone had bought a single new decoration in years. The same age-old baubles and knick-knacks adorned the fake pine tree. There was even the Christmas cracker she had made in primary school hidden on the boughs. Outdated tinsel and trailing ceiling garlands brought back memories of happier times. But Kate was anything but happy.   Her life had fallen apart. Paul, her boyfriend of five years, had packed his bags ten days before. He told her he was leaving her for a Spanish señorita, a waitress he had met three months earlier and they were travelling to Tenerife to start a new life together. Paul left Kate with a broken heart, a rent bill she couldn't pay, her dog Sunday, and an ever-increasing mountain of debt.

The lack of funds had forced her back to her parents' house and, if she was being honest, she didn't think either of them was overly happy about her return.

The front door opened and quickly slammed shut.

'Burrh! It's cold enough to freeze the balls off a brass monkey out there!' Alan, Kate's dad, bellowed from the doorway.

She heard his boots brushing snow onto the doormat. 'Easy, Sunday. You can see your mum in a minute... when she comes to dry your feet.' His voice rose toward the end of his sentence, hinting at Kate's participation.

His daughter sunk further into the armchair, her forehead almost touching the tall G&T glass. An exasperated sigh escaped her lips.

'Leave it to me, Alan,' Dorothy, her mum shouted from the kitchen and walked down the hallway. 'You know she won't do it. She's down in the dumps, wallowing in self-pity. Here,' she passed Alan an old towel. 'I've brought you this from under the sink. That will have to do.'

Alan nodded. 'Come here, boy.'

Kate experienced a moment of guilt. Letting her dad see to her dog's needs was pushing the boundaries a little too far.

The living room door opened and in charged Sunday. (So called because Kate had found him wandering the streets one Sunday morning. The owners never materialised, which was a good thing, as Kate had fallen in love with him immediately and couldn't have parted from him.)

Dorothy stood in the doorway, eyeing her daughter with a hint of derision, while Kate ignored her daft dog as it ran around the room. Much too close to the Christmas tree for Dorothy's liking.

'It's no good sitting there feeling sorry for yourself, young lady. It's about time you pulled yourself together. Just look at you! Still in your pyjamas in the early evening. It's not right. What would the neighbours think?'

'Leave me alone, Mum!'

'No! Now you listen to me, Kate Massey. Your father and I have had ten days of you moping around the house. 'Enough is enough.' She looked at Alan for support. He stood behind her, and nodded his head, but looked a little sheepish.

'Okay, so Paul's left you. And yes, that's awful, especially in December, but life goes on. You've got to buck yourself up and get back out there.'

Kate turned her head and glared at her mother. 'And do what, exactly?'

It was her mother's turn to sigh. 'Find yourself a job for a start. Get back in contact with your school friends. Surely one of them could help you out. I mean, you're not helpless. There must be something you could do. Especially at Christmas. Businesses are always looking for extra staff over the holidays.'

'That's true,' Alan replied. 'For quite a few years, when you were a kid, I helped at the post office at Christmas time.'

Kate groaned. She couldn't think of anything more boring than sorting through piles of letters and parcels.

'Yeah, right! I'm bound to meet the man of my dreams there! Who are you trying to set me up with, Postman Pat?'

Alan grinned. 'No, not him. I don't think Sunday would get along well with his cat. That relationship would be doomed from the outcome.'

Dorothy snatched the dirty wet towel, from Alan's hands. Now soiled with dirt and melted snow, she flapped it up and down as if she were starting an illegal drag race. 'That's enough messing about. I'm serious, Kate. You've got until tomorrow evening to find yourself a job, or I'll find one for you.'

'What? You can't do that!' Kate groaned.

'Just watch me!'

Alan and his daughter stared as she strode away.

Alan held up his palms and shrugged. 'You know she only wants the best for you, Jellybean,' he said, reverting to her childhood nickname. 'Don't let Paul win. You've got to move on.'

Kate squirmed in her seat. 'I know, Dad, it's just…'

When her eyes filled with tears, her father crossed the room to embrace her.

'Don't cry, Kate. You'll set me off! I hate to see you upset. Listen, every cloud has a silver lining. And everything happens for a reason.'

'Do you really believe that?'

'Yes, I do. Now, dry your eyes and come with me into the kitchen. Your mum's cooking her famous Toad in the Hole with onion gravy, carrots, and peas.' He rubbed his stomach and licked his lips. 'Yummy, yummy, yummy, I want it in my tummy!'

Kate laughed, despite her predicament. Her dad could always brighten her mood. She clambered out of the armchair, linked her arm through his, and they strolled toward the kitchen.

*

December 6th

'Kate! Breakfast!' Dorothy yelled up the stairs.

Kate groaned. It reminded her of her school days and her mother's early morning wake-up calls.

'Alison's here. Get a move on!'

Kate's groan lengthened. Her relationship with her older sister was anything but perfect. Alison was only four years older than Kate's twenty-four. Deep down, they loved each other, but their entire lives had been a constant circle of competition, fighting, arguing, and squabbling. They were polar opposites. Alison was married to James, a successful banker. They weren't short of cash, and she worked as a private detective, who was in constant demand.

In contrast, Kate had moved in with her wealthy boyfriend and had never worked a day in her life. To look at her sister, only highlighted Kate's failure. Not only in a relationship but as a successful member of the working world.

With a heavy sigh, she pulled back the covers and trudged along the corridor. Her shoulders slumped even further as she plodded down the stairs to the kitchen, dreading the interaction.

'Here she is!' her dad said with exaggerated enthusiasm.

Alison turned her head to look in Kate's direction. 'Hi,' she said, forcing the word through her lips.

'Morning.' Kate feigned a smile and plonked herself on a chair.

Dorothy turned from the stove with the whistling kettle in her hand. 'Coffee?'

Kate nodded. She couldn't shake the dreadful feeling that this was an intervention. Her entire family scrutinised her every move in silence.

Determined not to look scared or ask what was going on, she picked up the cereal box and pretended to read. Out of the corner of her eye, she saw her mother tick-tacking to her sister, urging her to talk. She also witnessed Alison's frown and heard the exasperated sigh she emitted before she spoke.

'So, listen, Kate.' Alison began. 'Mum says you're looking for a job.' 'Actually, I'm...'

'Yes, she is!' Dorothy interrupted. 'She's stuck in this house day after day. She needs something to keep herself and her mind occupied.'

'Yeah, thanks, mum. I can talk for myself, you know!'

'Well, that's news to me. You've been moping in that armchair since you came back, drinking your dad's gin!'

Kate rolled her eyes toward the ceiling and ignored her. She was grateful her parents had let her come back home, but she hated how, from the moment she stepped over the threshold, in their eyes she had become a child again.

Dorothy wasn't about to let the matter drop. 'Alison's come to take you out, haven't you, dear?'

Both sisters winced at the use of "dear". It induced in them cringeworthy memories of their childhood and conformity to their mother's every whim. It was a condescending reminder to the girls, and Alan too, that she was the matriarch, and they were all her underlings.   Alan patted Kate's arm. 'We only want the best for you, Jellybean.' Kate and Alison locked eyes. Both realised they would have to see this through, whether they wanted to or not.

'I know dad.' Kate squeezed his hand still resting on her forearm.   'Don't keep her waiting too long,' Dorothy snapped when Kate reached for a piece of buttered toast. 'She's a busy girl is Alison.' The condescending sniff expressed the unspoken remains of the sentence. (Unlike some people around here!)

Kate took a large swig of her coffee and chomped down on the toast. 'I guess I'd better get dressed, then.' She pushed back the chair and headed for the stairs.

The kitchen seemed unusually quiet as she mounted the stairs. She paused on one step, inclining her head toward the kitchen. *Were they whispering? Why weren't they talking?* Another sigh escaped her lips. She was the failure. The daughter with no job, no home, no man in her life, and no way of rectifying the situation. 'I'm doomed to spend the rest of my life here!' she mumbled.

*

From the driver's seat, Alison leaned across and opened the car door for her sister without comment.

Kate slid into the passenger seat and sat in silence as her sister pulled away from the curb. She wanted to ask if she could turn on the radio; the silence was deafening. It augmented the negative feelings between them, caused by mutual jealousy of each other through years of confrontation.

'So, what do you want to do?' Alison said, keeping her eyes on the road. Her hands clutched the steering wheel too tightly; a sure sign she was doing this mercy mission under duress.

'Me? I thought you and Mum had this all planned. I don't have a clue.'

A long pause showed Kate her sister was unsure how to continue.

'Look. I only agreed to take you out because it's easier to say yes than argue with Mum. You know that as well as I do.'

Kate nodded.

Another long silence followed.

Alison turned on the radio. A blast of "Rodolph the Red-Nosed Reindeer" only lowered Kate's enthusiasm for a day out with her sister. Her thoughts wandered to Paul. *Why would someone leave you near Christmas time?* she thought, even though Google had already given her the answer. Apparently, being dumped around the Christmas season was common. It made her feel slightly better that she wasn't alone. There were probably hundreds, if not thousands of people wallowing in alcohol and curling up on their sofas.

'I tell you what. We'll go to the job centre and see if they can help you out. At least that will pacify Mum,' Alison said.

'Okay,' Kate replied, not relishing the thought at all. She had the sneaking suspicion that was what the whispering had been about in the kitchen. Alison was pretending she'd just thought of it.

'Then we'll go for a coffee and a cake like we used to do with mum when we were kids.'

Alison's words pulled her little sister back to the present. Kate didn't know if her sister's comment was because she genuinely liked the idea or if it reminded her of better times, but it brightened her face and lightened their mood at the same time.

However, by the time they reached the Job Centre, Alison's smile had turned upside down. 'What are you waiting for? Just go in!'

Kate wrung her hands together. Nerves had got the better of her. 'Yeah, yeah, just give me a minute!'

Alison sighed, opened the door, and dragged her sister inside. 'Will you just do it? I don't want to be stuck in here all day. It's depressing!' She frowned at the crumbling grey walls, strip lighting that had gone out with the ark and industrial-style brown carpet under their feet. A wonky Christmas tree stood in the corner. It had a grand total of twelve baubles dangling precariously from almost bald branches. The aged strips of tinsel looked like someone had thrown them at the tree and left them where they fell. They hung down toward the floor as though they contemplated suicide.

Kate wandered around, with little enthusiasm, looking at the noticeboards and the jobs offered.

Alison wasn't prepared to wait that long. She headed for an

official worker and found out what she needed to do.

'Kate! Over here!' She beckoned her sister toward her as if she were miles away.

A blush coloured Kate's face. Everyone was watching to see who acknowledge the bellowing fishwife. *Some private detective!* she thought. *She stands out like a beacon on a lighthouse!* Kate edged her way across the room, hoping the attention would have waned and everybody would have moved on to something else by the time she reached her loudmouthed sister.

'Sit down. This is Mike. He can help you,' Alison said.

Kate's blush deepened when she saw who was sitting on the other side of the desk.

'Well, well, well, if it isn't Kate Massey from Our Lady of Lords High School!' The civil servant flashed her a not-so-endearing smile.

It was times like these when Kate wished she owned an invisibility cloak and could make herself disappear. 'I'm sorry, I think you've mistaken me for someone else.'

Mike leaned back in his chair, his eyes mere slits in his angry face. He pointed his index finger straight at her. 'No. It's you alright,' he said, crossing his arms across his scrawny frame and leaning even further back in his creaky chair. 'I would never forget your face, now, would I?'

Alison scowled. 'What's he talking about?'

Kate feigned ignorance. 'I honestly don't know!'

'Oh, yes, you do!' His chair fell forward, back onto four legs, toppling his straggly, lank brown hair into his eyes. He swished it back with one hand and stabbed a finger in her direction with the other.

'I asked you to the graduation dance, and you turned me down.'

Kate cringed. 'I'm sorry, I don't remember...'

'You humiliated me in front of the

entire school.' 'I'm sure that's an exaggeration,' Alison chipped in. 'Anyway, that's all in the past now, isn't it? So, we're looking for a job for my sister...'

As soon as they got outside, Alison burst into laughter and Kate fought the urge to thump her on the nose. She couldn't believe how humiliating the interview had been.

'Wait until I tell my friends about this. Ha! They'll never believe it!'
'It's not funny.'
'Ha, ha! Oh, yes, it is! Whoever heard of going to the job centre and getting an interview to be Santa's pixie? I mean, come on. That's hilarious!'
'For you maybe, but not for me,' Kate scowled.
'Look on the bright side. If you get the job, it'll shut Mum up. At least until after Christmas, anyway.'
Kate had to admit her sister had a point. She let out an extra-elongated sigh. 'I suppose you're right.' She turned to face Alison. 'Will you come with me? To the interview, I mean.' She couldn't admit her legs were already shaking at the thought of it.
Alison's face broke into the biggest grin. 'Of course. I wouldn't miss this for the world!'

The shopping centre welcomed them with a blast of warm air as they stepped inside from the freezing temperature on the streets. People carrying bags swarmed the doors, threatening to sweep her and her sister back outside.

Unaware of Kate's increasing anxiety Alison grabbed her arm and yanked her further inside.

'Where do you have to go?' Alison peered at the tiny card in her sister's hands.

Kate squinted at the information. Fear twisted itself around the butterflies in her stomach and squeezed them to death. 'I have to find the customer service department.'

Alison scanned the area in front of them. 'It's over there. Come on.'

Kate envied her sister's enthusiasm and self-confidence. It didn't seem fair their personalities could be so different. In contrast, she was quivering in her soaking-wet boots. 'Alison, can you do it for me?'

'Do what?'

'The interview. You're so much more confident and outgoing than me. And nobody would ever know. We are so alike anyway.'

Alison's eyes perused her sister as though she'd never seen her before. It was true they were both short and slim. They had long brown hair with a gentle curl on the ends and their facial bone structure was the same. The main difference was that Kate had vivid green eyes, like her mother's, that you could dive into, whereas Alison's were a brilliant blue like their father's.

'Please...' Kate tried to look as sad and pathetic as she could.

'No way! If I don't get the job, you'll blame me!'

'No, I won't. Do you think I'd care if I didn't get to dress in bright red and white striped tights and a green pixie suit throughout Christmas? Come on! You'd be doing me a favour.'

Alison scrutinised her sister's body language. Her eyes narrowed. 'Huh! Alright, but don't blame me if I get you the job either. Deal?' Kate shook her sister's outstretched hand. 'That's a deal.'   'Go for a walk around the shopping centre and I'll meet you by the café in the corner as soon as this fiasco is over.' Alison brushed her hair over her shoulders, thrust out her chest and marched toward the customer service desk.

Kate stood behind a large potted fern, watching as Alison got the information and strode toward her again. Her sister slowed down to a casual stroll as she approached.

'I've got to head to the manager's office,' she muttered through almost closed lips, reminding Kate of a ventriloquist. 'A Mr Daniels.' Alison rolled her eyes to the heavens. 'For goodness sake, stop hiding like you've committed a crime! Go to the café. Wait there!'

Kate was aimlessly stirring her coffee when Alison came charging toward her with a huge grin on her face. She threw herself into the opposite seat. 'You start tomorrow! Here.' She pushed a large plastic bag across the table.   Flabbergasted, Kate couldn't quite take it all in. 'What?'

'Ha! I got you the job!' Alison beamed.

That stopped Kate's incessant stirring. Her shoulders slumped. 'What? You're joking!'

'No. I'm being serious. Go on. Look in the bag.'

Kate peered inside.

'That's your costume! Green tunic, red tights, green curled-up boots and a pointed hat with bells on. They want you to plait your hair and they might give you some wire to thread through them, so they stand up.'

Kate looked appalled. She shrank in her chair. 'Please tell me you're joking, and you've bought this costume just for a laugh.'

'Nope, little sis. You are officially one of four pixies at Silver Springs Shopping Centre.' Alison grinned. She explained work schedules, duties and the location of the staff room. 'You'll have to work every day until the twenty-fourth because, after that, you'll be free! Now, I think you can at least say thank you and buy me a coffee for all my hard work.'

Kate grumbled 'thanks,' you and trudged to the counter. She supposed working every day for a couple of weeks would take her mind off Paul and her present depressing situation. But a pixie in a grotto! Her eyes rolled toward the ceiling. Trust Alison to drop her in it! *If anyone I know sees me in there, I'll never live it down!* She thought.

Little did she know what fate had in store for her.

'Oh, how lovely!' Dorothy preened. 'I'll have to come and see you. It'll remind me of when you two were both little girls. Your dad and I took you every year to see Santa Claus. I must dig those photos out and we can have a look.' She wandered out of the kitchen in search of the elusive albums.   Alison couldn't stop grinning. She revelled in her sister's discomfort.

Kate fought the urge to slap her face. It grew more difficult with every passing second.

'Hey, Mum!' Alison yelled. 'Don't forget to take some photos of Kate in her pixie costume this year.'

Alan chuckled. He recognised the growing annoyance on his younger daughter's face. Alison always knew how to burrow under her skin.

Dorothy came back with her arms full of photo albums. 'Oh, yes, that's a great, idea, Alison. Alan, why don't you make us all a nice cup of tea while Alison and I find the photos? Kate, go put your pixie suit on.'

Alison stifled a giggle while Kate rolled her eyes to the ceiling and sighed theatrically.

'Not now, Mum. I'll do it tomorrow before I go to work.'

'Now, listen to me young lady,' her mother snapped. 'You'll do as you're told and put it on now. What if it's too small? Then what are you going to do? Huh? Or it could be too big. Then you'll need to alter it. If you try it on now, we'll know, won't we?'

Kate sighed again. She put both palms on the table and forced herself to stand up.

When she snatched the plastic bag off the kitchen unit and headed for the stairs, Alison shouted, 'Don't forget the hat and the boots! They might be the wrong size too.'

Kate muttered expletives under her breath as she trudged up the stairs.

'Oh, you look so cute!' Dorothy clapped her hands together and smiled. The first one Kate had seen since her arrival almost two weeks ago.

Alison routed in her bag for her phone. 'Let me get your picture for the album,' she grinned.

'Yes, that's a great idea,' Dorothy agreed. 'Take a few, Alison, and we can pick the best one.'

Resigned to the impromptu photoshoot, Alison stood in the kitchen with a permanent scowl etched across her face.

'I know. Let's take some of you standing beside the Christmas tree. That will look even more festive,' Dorothy said, already exiting the kitchen.   Kate saw Alison poised to take another photo, so she stuck two fingers up and stuck out her tongue.

'Beautiful! That's the best one yet!' Alison quipped. 'Better not do that in front of all the little kids, though. You might give them the wrong impression.'

'Shut up.'

'Of course, if you'd braided your hair before you came downstairs, that would have made you look more authentic.'

'Why do you hate me so much?' Kate replied.

'I don't know what you're talking about. You're my sister. I have to love you.' Alison looked repentant. 'Okay, I admit it. Now and again, I like to see you in awkward situations. It's funny.'

'Not for me, it isn't.'

'I know. That's what makes it even more hilarious for me! You're so tightly strung. You need to chill out a bit. Experience a bit of real life.'

Alan took Kate by the elbow. 'She's right, you know. Come on, Jellybean. You better get in there before your mother loses her patience!'

Chapter two

Hi ho! It's off to work she goes.

December 7th

Kate sat on the bus, wishing she had thought this through. She'd borrowed her mother's long coat, which had gone out of style with the dinosaurs.

Underneath, she wore her pixie costume, but her red stockinged legs were getting a lot of stares and giggles from the other passengers. She supposed her hair braided into two plaits didn't help matters either. In her hand, she clutched the plastic bag with her pixie boots and hat. The jingling of tiny bells every time the bus fell into a pothole was also causing eyebrows to lift and smirks to appear. She was glad when it was her stop, and she could get off and lose herself in the bustling high street.

Even when she arrived in the staff room, the smirks didn't subside. She swallowed her embarrassment and introduced herself.

'Hi, I'm Kate. It's my first day here.'

'We'd never have guessed!' One young woman sitting on the sofa said. Sarcasm dripped from every syllable. She was around Kate's age, maybe a couple of years younger. She sat with her arms folded, trying to cover her ample chest. One leg pumped up and down at the knee, highlighting her annoyance at Kate's appearance.

'Gemma! That's rather unkind. Please be friendly and make her feel welcome.' The speaker held out her hand. 'Hi. I'm Carol. I'm part of the Christmas grotto gang, too.'

'She's our boss,' said a third young woman. She also sat on the sofa. In one hand, she clutched the seemingly obligatory cup of tea and in the other a packet of chocolate digestives.

Thirty-year-old Carol clicked her tongue. 'Yes, Mary, thank you. I was just getting to that. And please, don't eat all those biscuits yourself. They are to share!' She turned her attention back to Kate and frowned.

'When you did the interview, didn't they tell you there was a changing room?'

Sniggering echoed around the staffroom.

'Er... no, they didn't,' Kate seethed. She wanted to rip her sister's head off. She knew Alison would have planned this. Another embarrassing situation contrived to make her squirm and put her in the spotlight.

'That's unfortunate,' Carol replied. 'Don't worry. We'll show you where it is, so you won't have to travel to work, well...' she motioned the entire length of Kate's attire with a stroke of her hand. 'You know. Dressed like that.'

Kate felt a finger prodding her shoulder blade. She turned to face a pair of brilliant blue eyes and a white flashing smile that looked like it belonged on a toothpaste commercial. As she tried to take it all in, the owner of the handsome face shoved a mug of tea into her hands.

'Here, take this. I assume you take milk and sugar?'

'What? Oh. Yeah, thanks.' Lost for words, she couldn't draw her eyes away from the handsome stranger. His perfectly styled blonde hair highlighted his rugged bone structure. He was taller than her, but then most people were, and he had a contagious charisma that made her blush. Yet something told her he was probably dangerous. The type of man that chewed women up and spat them out.

'I'm Gary, and these two nutcases are Gemma and Mary.' The two girls giggled and waved, although their eyes were on Gary, not on Kate.

'And the old codger in the corner there, that's Brian. He's Father

Christmas.'

'Hey! Less of the old, you upstart!' Brian said with a chuckle. 'Any more detrimental comments about my age and I'll put you on my naughty list!'

'He should be on it already!' Gemma said, eyeing Gary with lascivious eyes.

Kate wondered if there was already some history there between them.

Both girls were about her height. Which she supposed was mandatory if they were going to dress up as pixies. Gemma, with the huge boobs, was pretty and slim and oozed sexuality. Mary was a little tubby and had a bad case of acne. They both had short black hair, probably out of a bottle, and enough make-up to warrant working as two drag queens in a West End show.

'So, Kate, what brings you to Silver Springs shopping centre and the Christmas grotto?' Brian asked.

Kate paused. She didn't feel like explaining her failed relationship to a bunch of strangers. Nor did she want to admit she was living back at home.

Gary saw her reticence and tried to lighten the mood. 'You could always sit on Santa's knee and whisper it in his ear if you like.'

Mary and Gemma guffawed as though they'd never heard anything so hilarious in their lives.

Kate knew they would slowly drive her mad if she had to listen to them both all day long. 'It's a long story. I'll tell you another day,' she said.

'Alright guys and gals. It's time we got a move on. We start in fifteen minutes,' Carol said, clapping her hands together. 'Kate, follow me, please. I'll show you where the changing rooms are, and I can designate you a locker.'

Kate took two gulps of the lukewarm tea and followed the others outside.

'So, this, as you can see, is the grotto.' Carol paused to let Kate's eyes feast on the elaborate spectacle. Several huge Christmas trees surrounded the outside of a gingerbread house. False snow littered the roof and in strategic places on the ground. Automaton reindeer nodded and brayed. Enormous, multicoloured lollipops and candy canes spun around in circles. A pile of enormous, impressively wrapped presents stood in the centre and a jolly snowman, liberally sprinkled with glittery silver sparkles, waved hello. Reams of red rope hung from golden posts to stop the most inquisitive of children from venturing where they shouldn't, and a host of Christmas pop songs played on a loop.

'Father Christmas sits inside the gingerbread house on his golden throne.' (Gemma opened the door so Kate could peer inside.) 'And your job, Kate, will be to keep order in the queue and open the red rope barrier to let each family through.'

Carol recognised Kate's dubiousness and patted her arm. 'Don't worry. You'll soon get the hang of it. Later, you'll be relieved by either Mary or Gary so you can do your spot.'

Kate frowned again. 'Sorry. My what?'

'Your twenty-minute Christmas carol sing-song.'

Kate's jaw dropped open. Her face converted into a scowl. 'I think there's been some sort of mistake. I can't sing for toffee.'

Her stomach tightened into a stranglehold and squeezed until she thought she might faint.

It was Carol's turn to frown. 'According to what the Manager, Mr Daniels, was told from the job centre, you worked the cruise ship circuit as a lounge singer.'

Kate's fingers curled into fists. *'MIKE!'* She hissed through her teeth.

'Pardon?'

'I'd rather jump in a bath full of custard than sing live in the shopping centre.'

Gary jumped in front of her. He still looked gorgeous even dressed as a silly elf. 'That could be arranged.' His eyes held a malicious beam of devilment that unnerved her.

Gemma glared at him. Mary giggled and Carol looked alarmed.

'Well, that may be, but you'll have to do the best you can today because we've got nobody to replace you.'

Kate felt her cheeks glowing redder than the two exaggerated bright red circles on her cheeks that Carol had insisted she create.

'I can't! I'd rather die. A cat with its tail caught in a door would sound better. Honestly. I can't subject the shoppers to that!'

Gemma emitted a sarcastic laugh. Mary grinned and Carol frowned.

Gary nudged her in the ribs. 'Don't freak out, Kate. I'll help you.' He flashed his winning smile again and for a second, Kate almost forgot what lay ahead. Then it all came tumbling back when the Christmas music started up and the others took their places.

Kate realised a small group of about fifteen people was already standing by the red entrance rope. Santa had taken his place in the gingerbread house, and Gemma and Mary rushed to take their positions by the door. Their lethargic swaying in time to "Jingle Bells" showed how little enthusiasm they possessed for the job.

The first couple of hours passed quickly. A steady stream of kids and parents joined the queue and waited to be allowed entry to see Father Christmas.

Gary, otherwise known as Elf Edelweiss, had performed a short magic act for the children. He finished by modelling balloons into flowers, dogs or aeroplanes, which he gave away to some children. A few cried when they didn't receive one. One four-year-old boy had a tantrum. He threw himself under the rope barriers into the snow, stamping his feet, crying, scrunching up the fake snow and throwing it everywhere. The humiliation on his parents' faces as they dragged him back in line made Kate vow never to have kids.

But the biggest embarrassment was yet to come.

Carol grabbed the microphone. 'Now, mummies and daddies, boys, and girls, Pixie Peppercorn will sing us all some Christmas carols. Are you ready kids?'

'YEAH!' they yelled.

Gemma nudged Kate in her side. 'That's you.'

'What?'

'That's your pixie name. Pixie Peppercorn. You've gotta go sing.'

Kate felt like her whole life had imploded to this moment of sheer mortification.

Carol beckoned her to the tiny stage, but Kate's pixie boots refused to move.

'Let's give her some encouragement, shall we? How about a round of applause? Hurrah for Pixie Peppercorn!'

Kate felt her legs inching toward the stage. She needed the toilet so badly, she doubted she'd even make it to the microphone.

Just when she thought her day couldn't get any worse, her eyes scoured the crowd. There, mingling in with all the shoppers, was her mother, father and sister! To say they looked appalled was putting it mildly. They knew she couldn't sing in tune. Alison had once said Kate's singing, played constantly, would induce criminals to crack and divulge their dastardly crimes within minutes. What was she going to do?

As the first few bars of Walking in a Winter Wonderland blasted through the speakers, Kate's eyes scanned the crowd again. Then she gasped. She couldn't believe it! Leaning against a pillar with his arms and legs crossed and wearing a smug expression of satisfaction was Mike from the job centre. This was payback time for her humiliating him.

Gary nudged her. 'Sing!' he whispered through clenched lips.

Pixie Peppercorn closed her eyes and sang the first line. When she dared to open them again, not only did she see most of the shoppers covering their ears and wincing, but her family was edging backwards, trying their best to escape the scene.

Mike was still there. The self-congratulatory expression of pure wickedness on his face showed he was enjoying every minute of her humiliation. He made direct eye contact, then fist-pumped the air with a triumphant grin plastered across his face.

Gary saw the interaction. He whispered to a passing security guard, then jumped onto the tiny stage and grabbed the microphone from the holder. 'Right kids. That's enough of that! Let's play musical statues!'

The kids cheered, then jumped up and down with excitement.

Gary turned to Kate. 'Quick. Organise the children with Mary. Gemma can man the entrance to the grotto, and Carol, could you take care of the music?'

Carol glanced in Kate's direction and cringed. She nodded at Gary and sprang into action.

A disturbance in the thinning crowd caught Kate's attention. Two security guards grabbed Mike's upper arms and escorted him away.

Kate didn't know what had happened, but she heard him proclaiming his innocence as loud as he could. Whatever it was, she felt a strange sense of retribution. He had set her up, but karma had played the final card.

Gary grinned to himself as the security guards marched Mike away. He was unaware what bad history the two had, but he assumed Mike must have perpetrated it.

The Christmas team slumped into the old saggy sofa and matching armchairs in the staff room, moaning of exhaustion and sore feet. Brian, who had been sitting down only complained of aching thigh muscles from all the kids crawling all over him.

Carol put the kettle on and threw some tea bags into mugs.

'I don't know about the rest of you, but I could do with a proper drink,' Mary said.

Gemma nodded. 'Me too. Why don't we all go to the Wheatsheaf pub?'

'Count me in,' Gary said. 'Are you joining us, Kate?'

Her hesitancy caused Gemma to comment.

'Maybe she feels awkward because she'll have to go out in those horrible red tights again.'

Mary giggled.

Kate glared at them both.

Carol intervened. 'There's no need for that, Gemma.'

'Come on, Kate,' Brian said. 'It'll be nice to talk to someone new instead of this sad group of reprobates.'

'HEY!' Gemma and Mary replied.

Kate glanced at Gary. There was something magnetic

about his enigmatic smile and his demeanour that hinted at wickedness. He reminded her more of a steamy vampire than a Christmas elf. Whoever had offered him the job clearly wasn't great at assessing people. But Kate was under no illusion. She still believed he'd be the love 'em and leave 'em type, but perhaps that was what she needed. A quick fling over Christmas to help her get over her ex and move on. Her hand fiddled with her glass of wine.

'Yes, okay.' She heard herself say.

'Great!' Brian and Gary said in unison.

Gemma and Mary sighed with frustration as they pushed themselves up from the sofa. Carol turned off the kettle and headed to the changing room for her coat. The others followed suit.

The pub smelled of spilt beer, soggy carpet, and sweaty bodies. A works' Christmas party was well underway. Women who once had stood erect and pristine in elegant eveningwear now wobbled on their high-heels and forgot to pull those annoying drooping shoulder straps back into place. The men resembled football hooligans. They swigged their pints, sang at the tops of their voices, and patted each other on the back after each politically incorrect utterance.

Kate regretted her decision to join the grotto group. She could have been halfway home by now, sitting on her own on the bus, staring out of the window, ignoring everyone. Instead, she was hunching her shoulders, trying to make herself invisible so she wouldn't get singled out. She remembered the bright red tights adorning her legs and pulled her mother's coat further around them. At the same time, she felt her cheeks searching to recreate the colour.

A hand cupped the small of her back.

'Don't look so worried. I won't let anything bad happen to you.' Gary whispered in her ear.

The heat from his words tickled her ear. She felt strangely aroused. Her eyes found his. 'Thank you.'

'No problem. Come on. Let's join the others.'

Her workmates had already commandeered a table and were shouting over the noise to a flustered waiter.

'I'll have a pint,' Gary said.

'Me too!' Brian replied.

'Kate, what do you want to drink?' Gary asked.

She'd prefer a G&T but wasn't prepared to pay city centre prices. 'A glass of white wine, please,' she replied, knowing that wouldn't exactly be cheap either.

'Just look at us!' Gemma said. With her permanent grin etched across her face, she fluttered her "come to bed" eyes in Gary's direction. 'We look like we're all members of Gary's harem!'

'Concubines,' Kate replied.

'Hey! Don't start using words like that in front of me!'

Kate's brow furrowed. *Uff! She's thicker than an Eskimo's sock!* She thought.

Gary tried to stop himself from laughing.

'Words, like what?' Kate snapped.

'You know what I'm talking about!' Gemma said, writhing in her seat with annoyance and narrowing her eyes.

Brian intervened. 'Gemma, do you know what concubine even means?'

'... of course, I do!'

'Go on then. Tell us.'

'It's a swear word. It means she thought what I said was rubbish.'

Brian laughed again. 'No! Silly. It means a secondary wife. In some countries, it's legal to have more than one wife. Apart from the first woman he marries the others are called his concubines.' He risked a smile in Kate's direction, hoping she realised he was defusing the situation.

'Ah! So, she's calling me a tart!'

Carol's voice rose above the banter and music of the noisy club. 'Gemma, for heaven's sake, Kate was making conversation. It's you that's blown everything out of proportion. Just drink your prosecco and be quiet!'

Gemma sat back and seethed. She felt sure Gary was fancying his chances with Kate. His facial expressions, the casual touch of his hand on her arm, and the whispering in her ear were all familiar signs. She knew them all too well, but once Gary had enticed Kate into his den and had his wicked way with her, he'd dump her quicker than a real Christmas tree after the festivities.

Gary couldn't understand what it was about Kate, but he felt the need to defend her, fight her corner, and keep her safe. Her vivid green eyes made her seem even more pixie-like. Her diminutive size, too. He had never experienced the attraction of wanting to be by a girl's side except to win her over and get her into his bed. Of course, that was still the plan, but he couldn't explain it. There was something different about Kate that fascinated him. She appeared lost, bruised and hurt, but he felt certain there was a feistiness about her he would love to bring to the surface.

A couple got up on the karaoke machine and warbled their way through a love song. Gary stood up and held out his hand. 'Kate, come on, dance with me.'

The look on her face showed her surprise and reticence. 'For a moment, I thought you wanted me to sing!'

Gemma and Mary guffawed into their drinks. Carol tried to hide a smile, but soon everyone was laughing.

Gary wanted to turn back time. She was giving him the brush off. He wished he'd never executed such an impulse act. She hardly knew him. Of course, she would turn him down. He felt Gemma's eyes boring into him. Laughing at his predicament.

'Go on, Kate. Pretty please?' he muttered, hoping Gemma wouldn't hear his pleading.

Kate didn't know what to do. Should she go with Gary and annoy Gemma even more than she already was? Or refuse him and end up in his bad book, or on his naughty list. *Did elves even have naughty lists?* She wasn't sure, but she had to decide. And quickly!

Determined to finish the day on a high, she held out her hand. 'Of course, I'll dance with you! Lead the way, Elf Edelweiss.'

'Come on, Kate, I'll drive you home.' Gary said when they all stepped outside, pulling their coats around them in a futile attempt to keep out the cold. A bitter northerly wind slapped their faces and tore at their hair while a faint sprinkling of snow fell on their shoulders and instantly turned into mush.

Kate was finally glad to be wearing her thick red tights. She looked into Gary's eyes. 'I think I'd better go home alone,' she said.

Gary's smile slid from his face quicker than Santa's sleigh coursing down a snowy hillside. 'Oh,' he said. 'it's no trouble. Believe me.'

Kate cringed. He probably imagined she had her own place, and he could take her back and seduce her on the sofa. Little did he know the reality of her situation. She could imagine it now.

Her mother and father would be sitting in the living room awaiting her return.

'Oh, you're back!' Dorothy would say. 'How was your day? Would you like a cup of tea?'

Her dog, Sunday, would charge around like the crazy mutt he was.

Alan, her dad, would converse with Gary about the most banal things until Gary had lost the will to live...

'No, it's OK,' she said. 'I'll be fine. Thanks for the offer, though. See you tomorrow.'

Out of the corner of her eye, she saw Gemma and Mary whispering to each other. The sparkle in their eyes showed how much they relished Gary's discomfort.

Gary shoved his hands into his pockets and shrugged. 'That's OK. No worries. I'll er... see you tomorrow then.' He sauntered away. 'Are you catching the bus, Kate?' Carol asked her.

'Yes, I am,' Kate replied, not wanting to admit she didn't have the money for a taxi.

'Great, I'll walk with you,' said Carol, linking her arm through Kate's. 'We girls must stick together,' she said. 'We shouldn't walk alone through the middle of Leeds so late at night.' Surprised by her action, Kate gave her an uneasy smile and nodded.

Gemma and Mary said their goodbyes and walked in the opposite direction. Brian had offered to drive them home.

Now was Kate's chance to get the lowdown on the Gemma and Gary situation. 'So, what's going on with Pixie Pumpernickel and Elf Edelweiss?'

Carol pulled her scarf tighter around her throat and stared into the distance. 'I, er... I don't think anything is going on. Well, not anymore.' Her top lip curled upwards. 'I shouldn't worry about it. Gary's a bit of a ladies' man. You know, the type that loves 'em and leaves 'em. Don't get me wrong, he's a great guy, but he's not looking for a serious relationship.'

'Yes, I thought as much.' said Kate. 'He seems like a good guy, though.'

'Huh! well, that would depend on what you're looking for, wouldn't it? If you just want a friend; someone to have a good time with, then you need look no further. But if you're looking for something more serious, then I guess he's not the guy for you.'

'Don't worry,' said Kate. 'I'm not looking for anything permanent. Just friendship.'

'That's good to know,' said Carol. 'Look. Here's your bus.'

Kate took a seat and then stared out of the window, assessing Carol's words. She wondered if Carol had also fallen for his charms and then been tossed aside. A sigh escaped her thinning mouth. What a Christmas concoction of mixed nuts she'd got herself involved in.

*

December 8th

The alarm rang. Kate forced her eyes open and scouted for her phone to switch off the annoying sound. Her brain was pounding on her skull with a jackhammer, her nose felt blocked, and her mouth tasted like the underside of a cattle truck.

'Kate. Breakfast!' Her father's forever pleasant voice floated up the stairs. 'It's your favourite. A full English breakfast! Eggs, sausage, bacon, beans…'

His words didn't have the required effect. She threw back the covers and bolted for the bathroom. By the time she'd finished throwing up the heady brew of alcoholic drinks she'd imbibed the night before, Alan was still reciting the final items of her breakfast.

'... toast, black pudding, mushrooms and fried bread!'

'Yeah, yeah, okay. I'll be down in a minute.' Kate stared at her greenish-tinged dishevelled image in the bathroom mirror. Mascara had crept down her cheeks like two long-legged spiders. Underneath the spider's legs, two black bags hung beneath her eyes. Her lips still held a faint remnant of lipstick in the grooves of her cracked lips. She looked dreadful.

'Morning, little sis!'

Kate jumped and spun around to face Alison. 'Don't do that! You scared me to death!'

Alison's eyes perused Kate's dishevelled body from top to toe. 'Good night, was it?'

'Uff! Don't ask.'

'What's up, Pixie Peppercorn?' Alison smirked.

'Don't even go there! Anyway, I've got a bone to pick with you. Why didn't you tell me there was a staff changing room? I traipsed through the centre of town with bright red tights on yesterday!'

Alison burst into laughter. 'Sorry. I forgot. Anyway, apart from your debut singing spectacular, how did the rest of your working day go?' 'Horrible!' She slumped onto the toilet seat. My life is such a mess! I've got to sort myself out.' Her thoughts went back to her ex-boyfriend. 'STOP!'

'What?'

'Stop thinking about your ex.'

'How did you...?'

'It's obvious. You get that faraway little girl lost look in your eyes. Listen. I know for a fact he won't be drowning in his own misery, so why should you?'

'I know, but I'm so out of my comfort zone I can't function.'

'So, what you're saying is you need my help.'

'I didn't say that.'

'But it's obvious you do. Do you know who you remind me of?' Kate shook her head. Then stopped. Her brain was swilling around inside her skull like a tiny boat in a rough sea.

'Pinocchio.'

'How do you mean?'

'You are gullible and need your conscience to tell you what to do all the time.'

'No, I do not!'

'Yes, you do. So, I nominate myself to be your conscience.' All in favour, say Ay? Ay! Great, so it's official.'

Kate's eyes narrowed. 'I haven't agreed yet. What have you got in mind?'

'Okay. So, you said you've got to pull yourself out of your comfort zone. You've spent the last five years living in Paul's shadow. He made all the decisions, and you did whatever he said. It's been that long since you thought for yourself, you've forgotten how to do it. You need to get out in the big wide world and get a life!'

'Well, that's easier said than done.'

Alison ignored her. 'So, here's what's gonna happen. I'm going to bug you.'

'You do that every time I see you.'

'No. I mean I'm going to put a bug on you. A microphone that will record every single conversation you have.'

Kate's eyes narrowed even further. 'How's that going to help me?'

'Because, from now until the stroke of New Year, whenever you're asked a question, you only have one option. You can only answer in the affirmative.'

'Can't you just say 'yes,' instead of your detective jargon?' Kate sighed.

Alison ignored her. 'Regardless of what the situation is, you must answer yes.'

'But...'

'The word "No" is no longer part of your vocabulary.' She saw Kate wavering. 'And there's more. A little incentive to help you agree to this.'

'What could that possibly be?' Kate's sarcasm didn't stop Alison. 'If you succeed. I promise you two things. First, I'll set you up in a small apartment so you can get out from under Mum and Dad's feet. And second, I'll give you two options. You can either work for me, or I'll pay for your first year at university. You've always had a clever mind, Kate. It's about time you started using it and began thinking for yourself.'

Kate stared at her sister, not quite believing what she had heard. 'Do you really mean that? You'd do that for me?'

'Yeah. You're my sister and I love you. I'm doing great with my detective work; my business has taken off, and I'd love to help you out.'

Kate wanted to cry. She couldn't believe her sister would make such a grand statement and do something so enormous as that.

She stared at her image in the bathroom mirror one more time. Pushing back her shoulders, she set her jaw. Her hands gripped the wash basin. 'Okay,' she said. 'I'll do it.'

Her lips cramped together in a harsh line, and a stoic jut of her chin showed her determination. 'I resolve to have a great Christmas and to hell with the consequences.'

Alison patted her on the shoulder. 'That's the Kate I remember and love. I'll see you downstairs.'

Her sister's words made tears prick the backs of Kate's

eyes. Perhaps her sibling wasn't so bad after all.

After giving her face a quick wash, she strode with determination into her bedroom and threw on some clothes. She dragged a brush through her tousled hair, slapped a bit of blusher onto her cheeks and added a pale pink lipstick to her cracked lips. Kate stared at her image once more. 'Go get 'em, girl,' she said. 'Let's make this a Christmas to remember!'

She was about to leave her room when her sister appeared in the doorway.

'Here,' Alison pulled a gold-coloured necklace from her pocket and fastened it around her sister's neck. 'Wear this at all times. It holds a hidden microphone and will record every word you say.'

Kate examined the locket hanging on the chain. 'Does it open?'

Alison shook her head. 'Don't even try. The microphone is inside. If you open it, the listening device will disintegrate and our deal will be off, okay?'

Kate smirked and searched her sister's eyes, looking for signs of mockery. 'Don't tell me you expect me to believe that!'

'Kate, in my business you can never be too careful. I'm like a spy. I need to be able to protect myself from detection. The only time you can remove it is if you're in the bath or shower.'

'Huh! I would have thought the genius who invented this device would have made it waterproof.'

'Yeah, well, they didn't, so be careful with it!' She patted Kate on the shoulder. 'Okay, you're all set, little sis. Your challenge starts now! You have until the stroke of midnight on New Year's Eve to say yes to everything.' She held out her hand and Kate shook it.

'You're on!'

Her mother frowned when Kate entered the kitchen. 'My goodness what's happened to you?' She asked. 'You look like death warmed up!'

'No, I don't,' Kate argued.

Alison gave her sister a condescending smile. 'Er... yes, you do!'

'What happened last night?' Her mother asked.

'None of your business,' Kate replied.

'Kate!' Dorothy snapped. 'There's no need to speak to me like that. I'm asking as a concerned mother!'

'She went out for a few drinks with her workmates,' Alan said, forever being helpful.

'Huh! Some mates!' Alison replied, stuffing half a sausage into her mouth. 'I'm surprised you even got home at all!'

Kate scowled at her sister. 'Well, obviously I did because I'm here, aren't I? Anyway, how would you know?'

Her sister shrugged. 'I just do.' (She couldn't let Kate know she had carried out surveillance on her all night long to make sure she was safe. That was why she had slept in her old bedroom last night. She had been too tired to go back home.)

'What time do you start work today, Kate?' Dorothy asked.

'I have to be there at ten o'clock, but I don't start working till later. We have pre-schoolers in the morning, then we get extra busy once the primary students finish school for the day.'

'How lovely,' Alan said. 'I'd love to see all the little faces. They must be so happy at the thought of seeing Father Christmas and all the elves and pixies.'

'We've only got one elf,' Kate explained. 'The girls are pixies the boys are elves.'

Alison's eyes narrowed. 'Yeah, I've heard about your elf.'

'Oh, here we go!' Kate shook her head.

'The word on the street is he's a bit of a ladies' man. Rumour has it, he's never seen out with the same woman twice.'

'The word on the street!' Kate quipped. 'He's working as an elf, not robbing banks!'

'Oh, dear me!' Dorothy exclaimed. 'A gigolo in Santa's grotto that sounds obscene.'

Kate rolled her eyes towards the ceiling. 'Mother, he's dressed as an elf. How many women do you think will fall for his charms when he's wearing a bright green costume, brown turned-up shoes and a hat with a big bell on it?'

Alison giggled into her breakfast.

Kate scowled.

Dorothy sniffed, knowing her daughter had made a valid point. 'Be careful, that's all I'm saying. Your track record with members of the opposite sex has always been a bit wobbly, hasn't it Alan?'

'Well, I've always liked the guys she's brought home.'

Dorothy clicked her tongue. 'Oh, just eat your breakfast. You're no use at all!' She turned to Kate. 'I don't want you making any silly mistakes. Will you promise me you'll be careful?'

Kate smiled. This was her first closed question. She had no other option than to answer in the affirmative.

She made eye contact with Alison. 'Yes!' she said, with rather more determination than was necessary.

Her mum smiled. 'That's a good girl.'

Alison stuffed fried bread soaked in egg yolk into her mouth to stifle her laughter.

Chapter Three

All I want for Christmas is Poo!

From the sofa, Gemma glared at Kate when she walked into the staff room. 'Oh, here she is, the floozy who wants to take my man.'

Kate turned around to see who was behind her, not quite believing Gemma was referring to her.

'I mean, you!' Pixie Pumpernickel jumped to her feet and pointed an accusatory finger at Kate.

'Me? I don't know what you're talking about,' Kate replied. 'Don't play daft with me. I'm talking about Gary. You want him, don't you?'

For the first time since her declaration in the bathroom, Kate doubted her decision. She fingered the locket. If she replied in the positive, this could lead to a fight, but if she didn't, she'd be stuck living with her parents for who knew how long! A frown danced across her forehead. Her mouth twitched as she fought not to reply.

'Yes!' she said. The word barely escaped from between her lips. Carol who was preparing cups of tea, swung around. Her mouth hung open, and the soggy tea bag dripped on the carpet. Mary who was on the sofa examining her spots in a hand mirror gasped and stared at Kate as if she'd just grown a pair of fairy wings. 'I knew it!' Gemma thumped the sofa seat. 'I'm telling you now, stay away from him. He's mine!'

'Fine by me!' Kate snapped.

Carol returned to the mugs of tea. She grabbed the nearest one and strode toward Gemma.

'Here. This is for you,' she said, hoping the girl would forget about fighting with a hot beverage in her hands.

'Did you hear that, Carol? She's after my man!'

'Listen Gemma... and don't take this the wrong way,' Carol replied. Realising she'd just armed Gemma with a red-hot liquid projectile, she got as far away from Pixie Pumpernickel before she finished her sentence. 'But the thing is, he wasn't exactly all over you last night, was he?'

'Of course not! Because she commandeered him, didn't she?' Gemma jumped up and slammed the mug down onto the table. The contents slopped over the side and puddled like a bloody crime scene photo.

Kate exhaled. The thought of spending the next several hours with Gemma was enough to make her think of ways to silence her. Like, tie the girl to the nearest chair and stuff her face so full of Christmas cake she couldn't say another word until their shift was over.

'Listen, I don't want any trouble. I'm here to do a job and that's that. I'm not looking for a relationship. You can have him, but I'm not about to ignore him just because you're jealous.'

'Who's jealous?' Gary's deep voice made her jump. Gemma tensed, and Mary stopped picking at her spots.

Carol walked toward him and handed him a mug. 'Here, Gary, this is yours.'

'Thanks,' he stood in the doorway, waiting for an explanation. 'Who's jealous of whom?'

Kate realised there was a slight flaw in Alison's plan. She couldn't reply to every question with a yes or a no. Open questions, like 'What time is it?' And 'Where are the toilets?' would have to be answered with a more complete response. That could be a good thing. Maybe she could rectify the situation. Or make it worse. But either way, she'd have to try.

'It's nothing, Gary,' Kate replied. 'Gemma's annoyed. She wants me to leave you alone because you're her boyfriend. She thinks I fancy you.' Gary's eyes narrowed. He flicked an annoyed glance in Pixie Pumpernickel's direction. Then, with a hint of a smile, he addressed Kate. 'And do you fancy me?'

Kate cringed! She was back in the same position as before. *Poo! Why didn't I stop one sentence earlier?* 'Er... yes.' The almost silent words barely slipped through her thinning lips.

'I knew it!' Gemma punched the table again. The puddle of cooling tea became airborne and crashed back to the tabletop.

Gary grinned. 'Then, that's okay, isn't it?'

Kate swallowed. 'Yes.' The words were so faint she hardly heard them. She imagined Alison in her office laughing her woolly socks off at her discomfort.

'I told you, Gemma,' Mary said. 'We knew she was trouble, didn't we?'

Kate had heard enough. 'Mary, don't you start. This has nothing to do with you. And please, stop picking your face or we'll have to change your name to Pixie Pimple Face!'

Gary let out a hearty laugh that caused Kate's face to break into a grin. Carol sniggered but hid the noise by stirring a teaspoon around another mug of tea.

'That's cruel!' Gemma replied. 'She can't help it if she's got spots, can she?'

'YES! She can,' Kate yelled. 'She can change her diet. Stop eating so much chocolate and eat more fruit. That would be a start.'

'Oh, right? Listen to "Miss Know-it-all." Who do you think you are? A dietician or something?'

Kate swallowed. 'Yeah! I am. That's right,' she replied, almost revelling in the situation.

That silenced her adversary.

I can't lose my job for impersonating a dietician, can I? She asked herself.

'Ladies, please! Let's stop this bickering and get ready for work.' Carol took a huge gulp of warm tea. Sometimes she hated being in charge. The extra fifteen pounds in her pay packet didn't seem worth all the hassle to babysit these young adults (she used the words lightly). They acted like high school teens squabbling over their first crushes.

Gary sauntered past the group, grinning and humming to himself. He loved being the cause of the upset, but he still couldn't deny he had different feelings for Kate than for anyone he'd met before. If someone had asked him to explain, he couldn't, but she had even haunted his dreams last night – and not in a bad way. Although, it surprised him she had admitted her feelings for him. He'd only known her for two minutes, yet it seemed out of character. She was more reserved than that.

Positioned at the grotto, Kate had plenty of time to people-watch. She enjoyed the expressions of surprise and delight on the younger children's faces. Some showed their reticence to approach the bearded stranger in the big red suit. Others appeared fine, then burst into tears when they got closer. Whereas slightly older kids sauntered inside as if they were meeting an old friend.

Gemma and Mary stood on either side of the gingerbread house with their arms folded across their chests. They were supposed to be dancing, but they flashed looks of pure hatred whenever she caught their eyes.

She felt a tugging on her tunic.

'Are you a real pixie?' The tiny voice dragged Kate back to the present. A little girl around four years old stared up at her.

'Yes, I am.'

'But I thought pixies were small. Tinier than me. Aren't you too big to be a real pixie?'

'Yeah.' Kate saw the child's mother frown. 'But you know all pixies are magic, right?' she whispered.

'Uh, huh.'

'Well, there's your answer. We pixies make ourselves bigger so the mummies and daddies can see us. When they do, it reminds them to bring their children to see Santa. If not, you wouldn't be able to tell Father Christmas what you want for Christmas.'

'Oh! I get it.'

'Good!' Kate replied because she wasn't so sure she understood it herself.

'Is he nice, Santa?'

'Yes. He's gentle and kind, and he loves children.'

'Good. Will he let me have a puppy for Christmas?' The frantic, negative shaking of her mother's head made Kate's intestines twist.

'Yes, he will.'

The mother let out an exasperated sigh and glared at Pixie Peppercorn. 'Thanks a lot!' She snatched her daughter's hand and stomped into the gingerbread house.

'What was that all about?' Carol stood with her hands on her hips. 'What just happened?'

'I'm sorry. The mum got annoyed when I told her daughter she'd get a puppy for Christmas.'

The force of Carol's intake of breath made Kate fear she was going to be sucked inside Carol's mouth and disappear forever.

'You can't say things like that. Can you imagine that poor child on Christmas day?'

'Yes.'

She'll be so disappointed!'

'I know. I'm sorry. It won't happen again.'

Carol exhaled to show her annoyance. 'Change places with Mary. Stand by the gingerbread door and dance to the music.'

'No, please. I can't stand so close to Gemma. That's a recipe for disaster!'

Carol was beginning to believe Kate was a *total* disaster. It wouldn't matter where she was positioned. She sighed again with exaggeration. 'I don't have time for this, Kate. Stand over there, by the door, and don't talk to anyone.'

'Will you come with me and...'

Carol sighed again. 'Yes, now come on!'

Pixie Pumpernickel and Pixie Petunia (Mary) grumbled and complained about being split up.

Gary sauntered over to break it up and use the situation to his advantage. 'Carol, why doesn't Kate stand with me? Then Gemma and Mary can stay together.'

'No!' Carol snapped. 'Then I'll have the whole team chatting among themselves! You are all here to work. Gary, go back to your spot. Mary and Kate change places.'

Kate stood beside the door, avoiding looking in Gemma's direction. 'Oh, that's just great!' Pixie Pumpernickel snapped. She turned away from Kate and folded her arms across her ample chest.

'Gemma! Will you stop sulking?' Carol hissed. 'Honestly!

It's like babysitting toddlers! The customers are watching. Get back to work, all of you. We'll talk about this when we've finished the shift.'

Kate couldn't remember ever dancing to "Jingle Bells" and "Little Donkey" in her entire life, and she wasn't about to start now. While Gemma moved and squirmed more like a pole dancer rather than a pixie, and not at all in keeping with a kids' grotto, Kate resorted to striking daft poses and pulling silly faces.

The kids loved it. They grinned, giggled, and clapped at her silly antics.

When a father asked to have his child's photo taken beside her, Kate had to answer in the affirmative.

The man gave her a pound tip. 'Thanks. You've made my son's day.' Kate grinned. 'Thank you. The pleasure was all mine!'

Gemma clicked her tongue, tossed her head, and rolled her eyes to the ceiling. 'Typical!'

Kate ignored her, but their boss, Carol, had seen an opportunity. This could entice more people to come to the grotto. Visions of a small photo area, probably at the entrance to the entire grotto would entice more kids to pester their parents to go inside. Kate looked cute in her pixie outfit. Carol imagined groups of teenage boys and young men fighting to get a photo.

Maybe she could alternate between the three girls. Gemma, with her enormous breasts, was bound to attract members of the opposite sex. Mary was more of a challenge, but perhaps Carol could persuade her to wear a full costume. A snowman or a reindeer came to mind. No! The Grinch. That would be a good one!

Gary stood watching the impromptu photo. Mary stood at his side, monitoring him.

'You like her a lot, don't you?'

Gary turned to look at her spotty face, unsure whether to tell her the truth or lie. She'd probably blab his words to Gemma the first chance she got. Although that might not be a bad thing if it got Pixie Pumpernickel off his back.

'Yeah, Mary, I do.'

'But why? What's she got that Gemma hasn't?'

'I don't know,' she's different, that's all.' He could have given her a string of reasons, but he stopped himself. One, because she wouldn't remember them all. Two, those she did recall she'd tell Gemma, who wouldn't like any of them. And three, he needed to keep Gemma on his good side, so he had her to fall back on if his plans didn't come to fruition.

'But how is she different? It doesn't make sense.'

Gary sighed. 'Never mind. Why don't you help me entertain the kids? I can do my magic tricks and you can be my assistant.'

'Cool!' Mary replied. 'What do I have to do?'

When Kate got back home, she grabbed Sunday's lead and yelled to her parents she was going out. Work today had worn her down. Gemma had been a constant pain in the backside. Mary spent the entire afternoon either glaring at her or gracing her with a knowing smirk. (What she knew was up for debate.)

Carol had bored them all with a reprimand for their behaviour in the grotto. She then informed all three pixies they would now have to do photoshoots during each shift.

Kate guessed it was better than trying to sing karaoke Christmas songs, but it wasn't something she relished.

Sunday pulled on the lead, reminding Kate they were outside in the chilling cold air, and he wanted to be free. But Kate couldn't let him off in the residential area. The dog stopped to sniff a steaming pile of excrement, but Kate was oblivious to the situation. Her mind was still running through the events of the day.

'HEY! You! Is that your dog?'

Kate remembered her sister's challenge and wanted to die. If she answered in the affirmative, she would plunge herself into a confrontational showdown. But she had no other option. She braced herself for the fallout.

'Yes.' Her eyes fell on an irate old age pensioner with a face like a wrinkled sultana. The remains of his thinning hair flicked around his face in the growing wind. He brandished a fist in her direction.

'Then clean up that mess! I'm sick and tired of cleaning up after your hound!'

'That's not my dog! I mean, it is my dog. It's not my dog's mess.'

'Don't pull that one on me, young lady. It's still steaming! Of course, it's yours.'

'I'm telling you; it isn't.'

'I know your type. You think you're too good to pick up after your dog, don't you?'

Kate's fingers curled into fists and her stomach twisted into a knot. 'Yes,' she almost whispered.

If he heard, he didn't react. He was too busy ranting. 'Well, let me clarify something for you. You're not. I bet you haven't even got a doggy bag to pick it up with, have you?'

'Yes.' She dug her hands into her jacket pockets, trying to locate a carrier bag, but all she found was a used tissue and that day's bus ticket. She visualised the plastic bag sitting on the kitchen table where she had left it. 'I...'

'You're right, sir,' a male voice shouted from across the street.

'I've seen her before. She never picks up after that dog.'

Kate turned and glared at her nemesis. Civil servant Mike stood on the opposite curb. She could sense his pleasure at her discomfort radiating toward her.

'Go away, Mike, and mind your own business.'

'I'm sorry, but this is my street, so where you let your dog go to the toilet concerns me.'

'Are you going to pick it up?' the neighbour glared at Kate.

'Yes.' Kate replied, sticking to her vow, and hating every minute. 'But I seem to have lost my bag. I don't suppose you could lend me one?'

'Lend?' He laughed and turned toward Mike. 'Did you hear that? Lend, she says!' He swung around to face Kate. 'I'm hardly likely to want it back when it's had poop in it, am I?'

'Look I've not had the best of days, and this takes the biscuit. Are you going to give me a bag or not?'

'Wait there,' he replied and stomped up his driveway towards the house.

'So, you've only been back ten minutes and you're already annoying the neighbours. That's not a great start, is it?' Mike said. Sarcasm dripped from every syllable.

'Yes, it is,' she said, thinking her response made little sense. 'But you should know. You've been annoying people from the moment I first clapped eyes on you.'

'Here you are,' the neighbours waggled a supermarket carrier bag in front of her face.

His actions cleared her mind. Her deal may have forced her to say yes, but she could always get revenge on Mike Abbott... and she'd enjoy doing it.

'You'll regret this, Mike,' Kate said. 'And you,' she said, holding out an accusatory finger in the other man's face. 'I'll pick it up. But I'm telling you now. This mess isn't from my dog! And when the truth comes out. I expect an apology.' With her hand inside the bag, she scooped up the steaming poop and walked away with her head held high and two fingers holding her nose.

Chapter Four

Christmas is cancelled!

December 9th

Kate now dreaded breakfasts in her parents' house. Her mother grilled her like she was a war criminal. Dorothy was determined to discover what her daughter got up to all day. 'What are your plans today?'

'Nothing much.'

'Where will you eat lunch?'

'At work, mum!'

'What time will that be?'

'About two o'clock. I've told you this before.'

'What time will you be home this evening?'

'Mum! What is this, the third degree? I don't know, okay!'

Dorothy sniffed. 'Excuse me! I'm only interested in my daughter's life. Is that so bad?'

'Yes!'

'Alan. Have you heard how your daughter speaks to me? After all we've done for her, this is the thanks we get!'

'She's tired, love. It must be hard work keeping all those little children entertained all day.'

'Hard work? Huh! She doesn't know the meaning of the word. Anyway, she only started two days ago.'

'Yes, love, but...'

'And she finishes work on Christmas Eve. That's hardly going to kill her, is it? Hard work is what *you* do, dear. Day in, day out, year after year to keep bread on the table. She's just playing at it!'

Kate jumped to her feet. The movement was so abrupt, that her chair crashed to the floor. 'Enough! I'm doing the best I can, mum! I'm sorry if it isn't good enough for you. But I'm trying!'

Tears sprang to her eyes. She ran from the kitchen not wanting her mother to see her weakness.

'Dorothy, she's doing her best. That scoundrel, Paul, has turned her whole life upside down. Give her a chance to sort herself out.'

Alan's words filtered up the stairs, following Kate. His comments filled her with even more sorrow. She had lost everything. Coming back home signalled her failure. Her emotions bubbled up inside her until she felt as worthless as the steaming lump of poop the angry neighbour had forced her to remove the day before.

After she had washed and dressed, her mother appeared at her bedroom door.

'Can I come in?'

Kate wanted to answer in the negative, but because of her agreement, she nodded, then added 'yes', in case Alison accused her of not following the rules. She didn't need any more hassle.

Dorothy sat on Kate's bed and patted it, expecting her daughter to join her.

Kate was reticent to comply. 'What do you want, Mother? I haven't got a lot of time.'

'I'm here to apologise. Kate, I'm sorry. You have gone through a horrible experience and perhaps I should have more compassion for your predicament. I know I wouldn't have wanted to return to my parents' house when I'd already left.'

'Thanks.' Kate forced the word through her lips. She was waiting for the "but". It didn't take long.

'But you need to think about the bigger picture, Kate. Working as a pixie is hardly your dream job. What would you like to do after Christmas?' *Win a million pounds on the lottery and get the hell out of here!* Kate screamed inside her head. She raised her shoulders in a hesitant shrug. 'Dunno.'

'Your problem is you moved in with your boyfriend and let him provide for you. Times have changed, Kate. You shouldn't rely on someone else to supply your needs. You should be the leader in your game of life.' Kate fought the urge to roll her eyes. Her mother always spoke with a creative flourish whenever she was giving advice.

'Will you let me help you?'

Through gritted teeth, Kate replied, 'Yes,' and imagined Alison laughing her head off in her office.

'Great! That's a good girl. Leave everything to me.' Dorothy patted her daughter's lap.

Kate wanted to counterattack. She wanted to ask how allowing her mother to organise her life was any different from her ex-boyfriend who had done the same thing. But, worried that extending the conversation she may have to agree to more of her mother's demands, she kept her thoughts to herself.

'I'll leave you to get ready for your little job.'

Kate wanted to scream and punch the wall. It might not be the job of a lifetime, but it was still demanding, as was every job! She galloped downstairs and grabbed Sunday's lead. 'I'm taking the dog for a walk!' she yelled as she slammed the door. Kate took a different route, steering clear of the street where the previous altercation had happened. The mood she was in if she saw Mike, she wouldn't need to set her dog on him, she'd do it herself!

*

'Oh, look it's the boyfriend stealer!' Gemma's seething tone did nothing to improve Kate's mood.

'From what I've heard you lost him yourself by sleeping with him on the first date,' Kate counterattacked.

Her adversary frowned. 'Who told you that?'

'Someone who knows.'

'I bet it was Gary. What a pig!'

Kate grinned. She had just assumed that was what had happened. She had learnt how to get under Pixie Pumpernickel's skin, and she loved it. Every confrontation boosted her confidence. She made eye contact and shrugged.

'You're such a cow!' Gemma slumped onto the sofa and folded her arms across her chest. She crossed her legs. The upper limb pumped up and down, showing her frustration.

'Morning, my little harem of pixies,' Gary said.

Mary gave him her best smile. Gemma glared at him while her leg thumped up and down even quicker. Kate shrugged and gave him a wily smile, while Carol, as usual, stirred mugs of tea.

Movement in the doorway caught their eyes.

'Oh, good morning, Mr Daniels. Can I offer you a cup of tea?' Carol gushed.

Kate assessed him with interest. So, this was the guy who had interviewed Alison and didn't know they had changed places.

'No, thank you, Carol. I don't have time this morning.' He clapped his hands together, then brought them to rest under his nose. He could have been praying, but Kate doubted it. The others recognised it for what it was. He was about to give them some news they would not like.

'So, two things. First, a children's charity has approached us. They want to bring underprivileged youngsters to the grotto for a Christmas treat. Second, the Head office is threatening foreclosure of the three shopping centres in the chain with the lowest number of sales over the Christmas period. In a nutshell, if we don't improve our profits and get more people into the centre, we could all be out of a job by January. So, put your thinking caps on and come up with some ideas.'

He studied the vacant faces of his grotto staff. Oblivious to the fact that, apart from Carol, they would all be out of a job in January, anyway.

Carol broke the building silence. 'Oh! What a lovely idea! All those poor children will get to see Santa and receive a little present.'

'Yes, Carol, it's lovely, but the fact we may soon be unemployed is rather more important wouldn't you say?'

Kate had a sudden revelation. She raised her hand as if she were in primary school. 'Mr Daniels,' her voice sounded tentative and shy. 'It's just an idea, but couldn't we start a collection of second-hand toys? You know. We could encourage the more privileged kids to bring a toy to the grotto that they no longer play with. We can tell the children they would be helping Santa because he can recycle the old toys and make them new again. Then Silver Springs Shopping Centre could donate all the toys to needy kids.'

Gemma snorted. 'How's that gonna help the centre?'

Kate glared at her. 'If we publicise it enough, people will want to get involved. They always feel more prone to donate to charities at Christmas time. I think people look at how lucky they are and feel more obliged to help those less fortunate than themselves. If we did a Toy Drive, they would have to come into the centre to drop off the toys. I'm sure once they were inside, they wouldn't be able to resist a look around the shops for that forgotten Christmas present they need to buy.'

Gemma folded her arms across her ample chest and clicked her tongue. 'What a stupid idea,' she muttered.

If her boss heard, he didn't comment. 'That's a great idea,' Mr Daniels grinned. 'Er… Kate, isn't it?'

She blushed and nodded. 'YES!' she said, remembering to be vocal.

'Excellent! I'll get our publicity department onto it. But we'll have to act quickly. Put posters up all around the shopping centre, things like that.'

'You could advertise in the local paper. Or, better still, do some advertising on social media sites, that will soon get the word out,' Kate said, warming to her idea. 'We could also run a bake sale. My aunt is a member of the local Women's Institute. Perhaps she could get them involved and you could split the profits.'

'These are fantastic ideas,' Mr Daniels replied. He stopped to study her for a moment. 'This is just an idea, Kate, but would you consider being "the face" for this project?'

Kate had no qualms about answering in the affirmative. 'Yes! Of course. I'd love to!'

From the couch. Gemma squirmed and mimicked, 'I'd love to!'

Unaware of the animosity between the two girls, Mr Daniels assumed she was offering too. He turned to Pixie Pumpernickel. 'That's kind of you, Gemma, but I think one pixie will be enough.'

'My grandmother loves baking,' Carol said, attempting to diffuse the building tension. 'I'm sure she wouldn't mind making several cakes and cookies for such a good cause.'

'That would be great, Carol, thank you!' Mr Daniels clapped his hands together again then opened them, palms facing towards the group. 'Right! I'll let you get ready for work. Have a good day, guys.' He turned on his heels and left the staff room whistling Frosty the Snowman.

Carol stood with a mug of tea in her hands, watching him go.

Garry grinned. 'I think Carol's in luuurve!'

Mary and Gemma giggled maliciously at Carol's discomfort.

'No, I'm not!' A deep blush crept up her neck and headed for her cheeks. 'If you must know, I feel sorry for him.'

'Why?' Mary asked.

Kate pulled out a chair and sat at the table.

'It isn't my place to say. Now, come on, let's get ready for work.' She headed for the door, but Gary blocked her path.

'Not... so... fast. We refuse to take one step further until you tell us what you know.' His hands landed on her shoulders. He turned her around to face the group.

'Go on, Carol,' Gemma urged.

Kate mimicked her. 'Go on, Carol.'

Mary giggled. 'That sounded just like her!'

Gemma glared at Mary. 'Shut up! You cow!'

'Hey!' Gary yelled, 'Can both of you stop acting like primary school children and listen to Carol?'

'I still don't think I should...'

'Do it!' Gary's normal carefree manner had disappeared. In its place was a frustrated aggressor who wanted to be obeyed.

Kate squirmed in her chair. She had never felt so uncomfortable. She hoped Alison was listening in to the conversation right at that moment. If things turned nasty, she hoped she could count on her sister to appear somehow and diffuse the situation.

Carol sat at the table, opposite Kate. She leaned towards them, and almost whispered, 'Mr Daniel's wife and child were killed in a car accident about three years ago. He was a broken man for well over a year.

He had to take a leave of absence from work because he couldn't cope. When he came back, he had lost so much weight, half of us didn't even recognise him.'

'Did he marry again?' Kate asked.

'Huh! No way. Once bitten, twice shy, I say!' Gary quipped.

No one found him funny.

'Gary, that's in rather poor taste under the circumstances,' Kate muttered.

Gemma came to his aid. 'Freedom of speech, Kate. He can say whatever he wants. It's not up to you!'

Carol stood up. 'Everyone, stop bickering. We're going to be late. Come on.'

*

A moody group of Christmas employees wandered into the changing room. Gemma and Kate ignored each other. Carol felt guilty about telling Mr Daniels' private life to the rest of her team, and Mary stood in silence, staring at the vivid green Grinch costume Carol expected her to wear.

'You've got to be joking! I can't wear that! If anyone sees me, I'll literally die!'

'That's an impossibility,' Kate replied.

Mary turned her steely gaze in Kate's direction. 'No, it isn't.'

'Yes, it is. Literally means something will happen without a doubt, exaggeration, or inaccuracy. And as it's a virtual impossibility for you to die just by someone looking at you. Your statement is incorrect.

Mary's glare intensified. 'Who asked you? Did you swallow a lawyer's textbook or something?'

'Yes, I did.' Kate cringed at her own reply.

'Wouldn't that also be an impossibility?' Gemma remarked.

'Yes,' Kate said through gritted teeth. 'But if by "swallowed" she means devoured every word, then yes, that is a possibility.'

Mary had lost interest. She picked up one sleeve of the furry green costume and her lips curled upwards in distaste. She turned to her boss. 'Carol, come on. Please! I can't wear this. It's horrible.'

Gary tried to stifle a laugh. 'She has a point, to a certain extent. I mean, I've never seen a short Grinch.'

'You know what, Gary? You're right!' Carol's voice rose an octave. 'Don't worry, Mary. Put your original costume on. Gary, you are now the Grinch.'

'Me? Why?'

Kate wanted to laugh at his horrified expression. 'Yeah, Gary, you'd make a great one! You're more physically built like the character.'

'I am not! Mary is. She's got his belly!'

Mary burst into tears. Gemma comforted her friend, and Carol rolled her eyes to the heavens.

'Gary. You've got two minutes to get that costume on before I find Mr Daniels and get you fired for subordination.'

Kate scurried outside and headed for her station. On the way, she met Brian already in his Santa suit.

'Hi,' she said. 'How come you don't put your costume on in the changing rooms like the rest of us?'

'I can't do with all the quibbling and politics involved. It's bad enough sitting in the staff room and drinking tea with them. No. I'm quite happy getting ready at home and driving here in my car. It's great to see the reaction of the kids when they spy Santa in a white Fiat Panda.'

'Kate laughed. 'I can understand that. Both the politics and the kids' reaction. They must think your sleigh's broken or something.'

Brian laughed. A good hearty sound that embodied the Santa Claus persona. 'I tell them I'm giving the reindeer a rest because they have a very long night on Christmas Eve.'

'I'd love to see their faces,' Kate grinned.

'I tell you what. I'll give you a ride home one night and you can see for yourself.'

'Great! I'd love that.' She frowned. 'Uh oh! Here comes the grotto crew.'

'Or the grotty few,' Brian quipped.

Kate giggled. 'I guess we'd better take our places.' She wanted to laugh out loud at Gary's angry face hastily painted a nasty green colour. His eyebrows knitted together in a furious scowl.

Mary looked slightly more pacified in her usual green pixie suit. Gemma had already thrust out her chest and was smiling at anyone old enough to shave.

Kate wondered, for the umpteenth time how she had landed herself in such a group of reprobates. She blamed civil servant Mike. One day, she'd seek vengeance.

Mr Daniels interrupted Kate's half-hearted dancing session at the door to Santa's gingerbread house. He did a double-take at Gary's impersonation of the Grinch. He was doing a good job. Gary pretended to steal the kids' schoolbags or tried to convince them Santa wasn't there, but they didn't believe him as they could see him sitting in the gingerbread house.

'Turn off that dreadful music!' Gary yelled still in character. He covered his ears as "Walking in a Winter Wonderland" blasted through the speakers. 'Christmas is cancelled.'

'No, it isn't!' the children yelled, loving every minute of the interaction.

'Ah, Kate, there you are,' Mr Daniels said. 'I need to pull you away. The posters for the centre are almost done. We just need a photo of Pixie Peppercorn holding up a toy and that should about do it.'

'Oh. I, er… of course.'

Carol intervened. 'Mr Daniels, it's just a suggestion, but couldn't she stand next to the big bag of toys we have in the grotto? I think that would look rather impressive.'

The manager looked at the display of toys in front of him. 'Yes, that would be perfect. Now, Kate, could you do the honours?'

'Yes, of course.' She felt Gemma's eyes watching her every move. Kate wondered if she had been wrong to correct Mary's earlier comment about dying from a single glance. Perhaps if Gemma hated her (Kate) so much a single venomous death glare could kill her!

Mr Daniels commandeered the official photographer and asked him to take the photos, but it was he, Mr Daniels, who told Kate how to pose. 'Great, yes. Perfect. Now tilt your head to the left. Look at the presents and look surprised. Excellent…'

Gary didn't like what he was witnessing. Mr Daniels seemed way too infatuated with Kate. He only needed one photo for a silly poster in the shopping centre. Now he was acting like a professional photographer and ordering her around. *I bet most of these will end up on his bedroom wall!* Gary thought. Well, he'd have to put a stop to the manager's soppy ideas. Gary had already started his seduction routine and wouldn't stop until he had bedded Pixie Peppercorn. Then the snooty manager could do what he wanted with her. Gary had planned on keeping her around over the Christmas period, to keep his bed warm and have a decent bit of eye candy to turn up with at parties. Mr Daniels could just keep his hands off!

By the end of the shift, Gary was ready to pounce. 'So, Kate, I hear there's a great romantic comedy on at the cinema this weekend. It's a Christmas-themed film. Do you fancy going on Saturday when our shift finishes?'

Kate grasped the bug around her neck. At that moment, she would have given anything to break her sister's vow and get out of the date. Gary made her laugh, but he wasn't boyfriend material. Her original plan of using him to have a good time had waned away. She was better than a one-night stand. Throwing herself at the first man who showed her some attention wasn't her style, and she knew it. But now she had a dilemma. The draw of her getting her own place and a cash injection were the only reasons that stopped her from saying no, even though her entire psyche told her to do so.

Alison would play back the recordings or may even be listening to their conversation right now.

'Yes, okay,' she said, forcing the words through her thinned lips. Gary smiled. 'Great. Shall I see you there at seven forty-five?' 'Yes.' Her fingers curled into frustrated fists.

'Or would you like to eat somewhere first?'

An exaggerated sigh escaped her lips. 'Yes.'

'How about the burger bar?'

Kate exhaled. Finally, a response she could expand upon. 'I'd prefer to eat somewhere that doesn't serve processed food. Let's go to that new restaurant called "Peepers." I hear they do great fish and chips.' Gary's heart sank. To eat there would be twice as expensive. But it would be worth it if he could charm his way into her heart and her underwear! 'Alright, he said through thinning lips. 'What time?' 'I'll meet you there, at six-thirty.'

'Great!'

'Oh, and Gary...'

'Yes?'

'Make sure you shower first. You've still got green make-up behind your ears and in your eyebrows. I prefer not to look at the Grinch while I'm eating!'

Carol and Mary giggled.

Gemma gave an exaggerated sigh. She threw her pixie boots into her locker, slammed the door, and stomped out of the changing room.

Chapter Five

The face that launched a thousand hits

December 10th

Dressed in a light blue chenille sweater, blue jeans and white Cuban heeled knee-high boots, Kate stood outside the Peepers restaurant cursing Gary. He was ten minutes late, and she was slowly turning into a snowman! A light feathering of snowflakes danced before her eyes in the yellowed streetlights. They landed on her shoulders, making her look like she had a serious case of dandruff. She flicked them off and wrapped her white sequined scarf around her neck, but it didn't combat the cold. Her fingertips tingled, threatening to cut off all feeling, and her toes had lost contact with the rest of her body ten minutes ago.

'Alison, I'm going inside,' she muttered into the microphone. 'Gary's got five minutes to show his face, or I'm going home.'

The restaurant welcomed her into its warm, central heated embrace. Low lighting with a pleasant orange glow filled the room with a calming aura. Christmas decorations hung from the ceiling. Swathes of tinsel mixed with holly hung in drooping swoops along the top of the bar, and a tiny Christmas tree stood at the other end. Christmas pop songs played in the background; loud enough to hear, but low enough to hold a conversation, and intoxicating aromas of food tickled her nostrils. She realised how hungry she was. The many diners appeared relaxed. They talked, joked and laughed, enjoying the ambience and each other's company.

A young waitress approached Kate. 'Hi, I'm Melanie. Welcome to Peepers. How can I help you?'

'Hello. I'm sort of waiting for someone. Is there any chance I could wait at the bar and have a drink?'

'Of course,' Melanie said with a lovely smile.

Once Kate sat nursing her G&T, she took in her surroundings. Envy inched its way up her spine at all the couples who only had eyes for each other. The longer she sat there, the more annoyed she became with Gary the Grinch. She had stopped looking at the door every time it opened. Her gin and tonic had taken the edge off. Kate no longer cared if he came or not.

'Kate?'

She recognised the voice but couldn't quite place it. She spun around. 'Mr Daniels!'

'Please, call me, Ivan.'

'Oh,' she felt a blush creeping up her neck and repositioned her sequined scarf to hide it. 'What are you doing here?'

It was Ivan's turn to look embarrassed. 'I thought I should go out. It's my birthday today. I guessed I should do something to mark the occasion.'

Kate remembered Carol's story in the staff room and felt instant pity for him. The thought of spending a birthday alone wasn't something she would relish. 'Good for you. Are you meeting friends here?'

Ivan's blush deepened. 'Er... no. It was a spur-of-the-moment thing.'

'Then, you must eat with me and Gary... if he ever turns up.'

'Oh, no, Kate. I wouldn't want to interrupt. Gary would probably want you all to himself.'

Kate bit her tongue. She wanted to say, *he doesn't deserve to have me all to himself the arrogant poo!* 'No, I insist. I'm not even sure he'll come. He's twenty minutes late already.'

Ivan's face brightened. 'Well... if you're sure.'

Kate grabbed the remains of her G&T. 'Come on, let's ask the waitress for a table.'

Gary arrived once Kate and Ivan had ordered their meal and opened a bottle of white wine. His face made no effort to disguise his annoyance.

'Hi, what's going on?'

Kate cast him a smug smile. 'Oh. Hello, Gary. I thought you'd stood me up.'

'I, er...'

'I didn't think you were coming. Then I saw Ivan.'

'Who?'

'Ivan! Mr Daniels to you. It's his birthday. I invited him to join us.' Gary's face hardened. 'Oh, really?'

Ivan waved and flashed a weak smile.

'Yeah, really,' Kate replied. 'Sit down. We've already ordered, so I suggest you call the waitress over and get something quick. Otherwise, we'll have finished before you've begun.'

The Grinch pulled out a chair and flopped onto it. His plan had backfired. He liked to keep girls waiting. It made them vulnerable and more appreciative. If they thought he'd stood them up, they were more inclined to give out at the end of the night. But his plan had backfired. Stupid Mr Daniels had whittled his way into their date.

Ivan peered at Kate over the top of his wineglass. He liked her. She had a spunky character and wasn't about to stand any nonsense.

Since his wife's death, he hadn't looked at another woman. He had vowed never to put himself in such a vulnerable position again. The pain was too much to bear. Yet, this snip of a girl aroused something in him that had laid dormant for too long.

When they finished the meal, he knew he should take his leave and let the young couple have some alone time, but he couldn't do it. He was ready to ruffle Gary's feathers and maybe show his own plumage. The night was turning out to be better than he had ever expected.

When the bill arrived, Ivan insisted on paying.

'No, Ivan. I invited you. And it's your birthday. We'll pay between us, won't we, Gary?'

Gary glared at her. 'Yeah,' he said through gritted teeth.

'No, I insist.' Ivan slapped his credit card into the server's hand. 'You missed the film at the cinema by staying all this time with me. It's the least I can do.'

'I don't think it's right,' Kate said when the server returned.

'Nonsense. You've made my sorry birthday a hundred times better than I imagined it could be. I thank you for that, Kate. Oh, and you, too, Gary.'

'Yeah, right,' the Grinch muttered.

The server appeared with the bill and Ivan's credit card. 'Sir, we are running a Christmas competition. If you're interested,' the waitress waggled a wad of tickets under his nose, 'the winner gets a seven-day cruise around the Mediterranean to celebrate the new year in warmer climes. What do you think? Would it appeal to you?'

As Ivan hesitated, Kate jumped in.

'Yes, I'll take three, please. One for each of us.'

'Kate, there's no need for that,' Ivan said, while Gary simultaneously replied, 'Nice one!'

'No, I insist. Happy birthday.' She handed him his ticket. He took it but pushed ten pounds into the server's hand. 'Keep the change,' he said.

'Ivan!' Kate grinned and tapped his arm.

'I insist,' he said.

The Grinch fumed in silence.

Ivan glanced at Gary's number, then Kate's, and then his own. 'Thirty-six, seven and eight. Huh! Thirty-eight has always been lucky for me. Let's hope it is this time.'

Kate's eyes sparkled. 'Just imagine a New Year's cruise in the middle of the Mediterranean. How lovely! Some lucky people will have the holiday of a lifetime.'

Gary jumped in. 'Yeah. We'd have a whale of a time, you and me, Kate. Thirty-six is a lucky number for me, too.'

'Oh. I thought you might take whoever you almost stood me up for this evening.'

'What? No. I missed the bus, that's all. I had to wait for another one.'

Ivan stood up. 'Well, you don't need to worry about that now, Gary. I'll take you both home. My car's outside.'

'Great!' Gary muttered sarcastically.

Outside, when Ivan said he'd drop him off first, Gary knew it had been Ivan's plan all along. Any hopes of getting Kate alone had melted quicker than the fallen snowflakes under his feet.

*

December 11th

Kate had taken two steps inside the shopping centre when a security guard stopped her.

'Kate Massey?'

'Yes?'

'Mr Daniels would like to see you straightaway.'

She frowned. 'What's this about?'

The guard shrugged. 'Dunno. Don't shoot the messenger!'

A creeping feeling of dread ran helter-skelter through her body. Was he annoyed about last night? No. That made little sense. He had thanked her for a lovely evening when he'd dropped her off at home.

She recalled how he had leaned toward her and then paused. She had wondered if he was about to kiss her. Not a gentle peck on the cheek to thank her for spending the evening with him, but a full-on kiss.

It hadn't happened. He'd pulled back, his face a mask of pain. 'Good night,' he said, a distinct snap to his tone.

Kate had smiled. 'Thank you. I enjoyed myself.' She got out of the car. 'Happy birthday, Ivan.'

Kate knocked on the general manager's door and waited. Spittle refused to be swallowed, and she felt sick.

'Come in.'

Kate exhaled deeply before opening the door. His voice sounded so authoritarian; It reminded her of visiting the headmaster's office as a child. She cleared her throat and opened the door.

'Ah, Kate! Good morning!' He flashed her a kind smile from behind his large desk.

All her worries dissipated in a flash. 'You wanted to see me?'

'Yes. It's good news. Don't look so worried.'

'What is?'

'Your idea for the used toy promotion is attracting a lot of interest. We have received so many charitable contributions already, that we're considering donating to other orphanages, too. Maybe even abroad, like the Ukraine and Romania.'

Kate grinned. 'Wow! That's great!'

'I've called you up here because the local newspaper is on its way. They want to interview you.'

'Me?' Kate's discomfort squirmed inside her stomach and made her feel even more ill.

'Please, don't panic, Kate. I'll be there to support you. Will you do it?'

'Yes,' she replied. What other choice did she have?

'Great! Go to the staff room and put your costume on. I'll come and get you when they arrive.'

Kate headed off. She felt uncomfortable leaving the grotto to the others. It felt as though she were playing truant. When she had come up with the idea, it hadn't been part of a plan to thrust herself into the limelight. It was bad enough having to wear the pixie costume in the shopping centre and put herself on view every day. Now, the local paper planned to immortalise her wearing it in the paper!

When Kate got back home, she refrained from telling her mum about the media event at work. It would be a surprise for her. She couldn't tell her dad even if she wanted to. He had taken the dog out for another walk. Recently, he seemed to disappear more and more. And for longer periods every day.

Alison was in the kitchen eating two mince pies with fresh cream and drinking a large cup of tea. 'Hi, little sis. Or should I say Pixie Peppercorn? How's it going?'

'You know how it's going.' Kate glanced at her mother, who was removing more baked goods from the oven.

'You're listening to everything I say,' she whispered.

Alison looked embarrassed. 'Kate, about that. I'm up to my ears in an important case right now, so I admit, I'm behind schedule regarding you. Don't worry, I'll catch up. This doesn't mean you can stop agreeing to everything.'

'I know. I know!'

'How's that going, anyway?'

Kate mused over her sister's question. She glanced across at her mother to make sure she wasn't earwigging. 'It's going better than I expected. I agreed to meet Gary for a date.'

'Kate! I told you. He's no good. He's a love 'em and leave 'em sort of guy.'

'I know. Will you hear me out?' she glanced again in her mother's direction and beckoned Alison to follow her into the living room.

Her sister stuffed the remaining mince pie into her mouth, swallowed a large mouthful of tea, and followed Kate out of the kitchen.

'What happened?'

'Gary was late. It was snowing, and I was freezing, so I went inside the restaurant and sat at the bar.'

'Then what?'

Kate smiled. 'Ivan turned up.'

'Who's that?'

'Mr Daniels. The guy who interviewed you for my job.'

'No way!'

Kate nodded. 'It was his birthday, and he was out alone.'

'Uff! That's sad.'

'In more ways than one. His wife and daughter both died a couple of years ago in a traffic accident.' Kate frowned at her sister. 'Wow! You're way behind on the recordings, aren't you?'

'Like I said, Kate. I'm working on a case. That must take priority. Go on.'

Kate told her sister about all the events of that night.

'It sounds like Ivan has the hots for you.'

'I'm not sure. I think he was about to kiss me when he dropped me off at home. Alison, I need you to listen to the recordings and tell me what you think!'

'I'll try. So, good old Gary got kicked to the curb. Ha! I bet he wasn't happy.'

'No, he wasn't. Especially when Ivan dropped him home first.'

Alison laughed. Then her face grew serious. 'Huh! If Ivan dropped Gary home first, that makes me think you're right. Ivan has a soft spot for you. Come on. Let's go back into the kitchen before Mum gets suspicious and comes looking for us.'

They entered a war zone. Sunday ran around the kitchen table chasing an invisible rabbit. Alan and Dorothy were involved in a heated argument.

'What's up?' Alison said, stealing another mince pie from the cooling rack.

'It's your father! Ever since Kate's come home, he's out with that dog more times than I can count.'

'He has to go to the toilet, love,' Alan argued.

'That may be. But you're out that long. He must need to go out again as soon as you get back!'

'That's why I take him out so often!'

Kate stayed silent. After her run-in with the angry neighbour, she appreciated her dad walking Sunday. She grabbed the dog's collar as he charged past to stop him from doing any more circuits of the kitchen table. 'I enjoy walking him, Dorothy. I don't think there's anything wrong with that,' Alan commented in his usual placid, lowered voice. 'What with Kate working, I thought I was doing her and the dog a favour.'

Dorothy's confrontational manner disintegrated. 'I'm sorry, Alan. I just worry when you're out that long.'

'Don't worry. I'll take my phone in future. Then you can check up on me whenever you want.'

'It's not that I want to know where you are every single second. I just fret that something might have happened to you.'

All four of them remembered the previous year when Alan had experienced a heart attack around Christmastime. He was home alone and couldn't get to the phone. Fortunately, Alison had popped in between cases and found him.

A silence fell around them.

'I know love, but I'm not overdoing it. And the doctor said it would do me good to take gentle walks.'

Alison defended her mother. 'Yeah, Dad, but that's the keyword, gentle. You can't go charging around the neighbourhood for hours at a time.'

Kate kept her comments to herself. She was also concentrating on the same word. Gentle. Her dog was anything but! He wasn't great on a lead. He pulled and tried to run whenever he saw something he wanted to chase, investigate or sniff. Her mind shifted. She realised how she could defuse the situation.

'Anyway, guys. On a brighter note, I've got something to tell you. Do you still get the local paper, Dad? "The Weekly News".'

Dorothy's eyes narrowed. 'Yes, we do. Why?'

'Oh, just because I'm going to be in it!'

'No way! Why?' Dorothy held her hands up to her face as if she were praying.

Kate explained her idea for the toy donations and Ivan's plan to make her the face of the event.

Alison made eye contact with her sister and nodded. Now, she was even more convinced the boss had a soft spot for Pixie Peppercorn.

Alan grinned from ear to ear. 'That's fantastic. Kate! Well done!'

'Yes, congratulations!' Dorothy exclaimed. 'And I've got some good news for you, too.'

'What?' Kate's smile slid from her face. She knew her mother was about to say something she wouldn't like.

'One of my friends from the knitting club has arranged for you to meet her son on a blind date. I said you'd do it. You will, won't you?'

Alison guffawed into her cold mug of tea, as Kate froze in shock and glared at her sister.

'What's your answer, little sis?' A huge grin adorned Alison's face.

Kate wanted to slap her.

'Yes,' she said with a heavy sigh.

Alison laughed again.

Dorothy frowned. 'Alison, what's got into you?'

'Nothing! Please, continue.'

Kate glared at her.

'Perfect. Tomorrow night, Kate, after you finish work, your dad and I will pick you up from work, take you home to change, and we'll all go out to dinner.'

Kate scowled at her sister. Alison's shoulders shook, and her face turned bright red as she tried to hold in her giggles.

December 12th

'Kate. KATE! Come downstairs!' Alan shouted from the hallway. 'Look at this!'

His daughter rolled over in bed and stared at the ceiling. What could be so important that her dad needed her to get up? She squinted at the clock. Half-past eight! Poo! She started work at ten today. She'd better get a move on.

Her mother's voice got louder and more coherent as she exited from the kitchen and got nearer to the front door.

'What is it, Alan?'

'It's Kate. She's in the paper!' Alan held the dog's lead with one hand and ten copies of the periodical in the other.

'Ooh! Let's have a look.' Dorothy wiped her floury hands down her apron and took the proffered newspaper. 'Oh, what a lovely picture. I wonder if we could ask for an actual photo from the newspaper?'

'I don't see why not.' Alan said, unclipping Sunday's lead. 'I'll give them a ring this morning.'

'That's quite a write-up!' Dorothy preened with pride.

'It sure is. Fancy that. Our little girl coming up with such a bright idea.'

'You know, what, Alan? We should frame this.'

Kate groaned as she pulled herself out of bed. Her only hope was if they framed it, they'd only bring it out at Christmastime. She didn't want it to languish on the mantlepiece all year round for the entire neighbourhood to see her dressed as Pixie Peppercorn. With a sigh, she trudged down the stairs.

'Kate, darling, look at your photo!' her mother crooned. She almost threw a copy across the kitchen table. The tip of her tongue stuck out between her lips as she concentrated on cutting another one out of the paper. 'It's a fantastic write-up, and you look so cute in your little pixie suit.'

Her daughter cringed. She dreaded looking at the photo. What her parents called a decent picture and what she did differed by a mile! With her top lip curling upwards, she took hold of the paper. Her eyebrows lifted in surprise. 'Huh! It's not bad, is it?'

'Not bad?' her father repeated, grinning so much his smile threatened to reach his ears. 'It's fantastic! A great photo and a fabulous story. Who would have thought our little Jellybean would have come up with such a successful way to help the underprivileged? You should be proud of yourself. That's quite an achievement.'

Her mother patted her shoulder. 'It certainly is. Well done. Kate. Now, you must admit that's got to be better than moping around the house. You are making a difference in your community.'

Kate's mind flew back to the angry neighbour and the dog poo incident. She doubted he'd think she was making a difference. Making a mess, maybe, but contributing to anything positive was a definite no.

'This deserves a treat.' Dorothy beamed. 'I'll make us all some hot chocolate and a piece of Yule-log Swiss roll for breakfast.'

*

Ivan grabbed Kate the moment she stepped into the shopping centre. 'Hi! Follow me. I want to show you something.'

Kate assumed it was something positive by the way Ivan grinned at her.

'Look!' he said when they neared the grotto.

Kate could hardly believe it. A small mountain of toys stood beside the gingerbread house. A line of twenty people stood waiting to donate, and the shopping centre was buzzing with clientele.

'Isn't this great?' Ivan grinned.

'Yes. I'm… overwhelmed. I would never have believed it would take off so quickly.'

'There's more. Follow me.' He took her elbow and walked toward his office.

'Ivan. I'm not sure now is the right time. I've got to get ready for work.'

'Don't worry. I'll clear it with Carol. This is important!'

Kate shrugged and followed the boss. If she could lose ten minutes without wearing her pixie outfit, it was time well spent. That meant there was less chance of her being recognised by anyone.

Ivan threw open his office door and marched over to his computer. 'I want you to look at this. You won't believe it!'

Kate followed him behind his desk, looked at the screen and gasped. Any hope of remaining anonymous was well and truly gone. 'I took your advice. We made a short film about your idea and put it on our social networking page. Look! The video has gone viral on Facebook, TikTok, and Twitter… or is it called X now?'

'Yes,' Kate said, holding in a groan. So much for not being recognised! There she was in front of the gingerbread house dancing half-heartedly to "Rocking Around the Christmas Tree", greeting the kids and pulling funny faces.

'Great!' she replied with as much enthusiasm as she could muster. 'I should get back…'

'Wait, there's more.'

Kate wasn't sure she could take any more. All she wanted was a quiet life where she could wallow in her sadness. Then she froze.

No! That's not what I want at all! She reprimanded herself. Since she'd agreed to Alison's terms and met Ivan, her life had already improved more than she could ever have imagined. *Do I long to go back to sitting on my mother's sofa and crying into a G&T? Too right I don't.* She steeled herself. *Bring it on!*

She stared into Ivan's eyes. 'What, Ivan?'

'I've had two calls this morning. One from a national newspaper who saw the video on social media. They want to interview us both. The other was from Tom Brenner's agent.'

Kate gasped. 'Not Tom Brenner the chat show host!'

'The very same!' Ivan's grin couldn't have got any bigger if he had tried.

Kate swallowed. 'What did he want?'

'He wants to interview us, too.'

'I don't know what to say.'

'They've asked us to go to the studios tomorrow afternoon. He wants us to appear before a live studio audience and it will be broadcast that night on his show.'

'Is this a joke?' Kate asked, not quite believing her little idea had exploded into such huge proportions.

'No. I swear this is true. I can hardly believe it myself. It's incredible, Kate, don't you think?'

'Yes, that's one way of putting it,' she replied.

Overcome with happiness, Ivan jumped up from his seat and hugged her. 'Kate, it was the best decision I ever made offering you the job in the grotto. Your idea has put Silver Springs Shopping Centre on the map.'

He took her hand and led her to the window where she could look down into the shopping centre. 'Look down there. Do you see, what I mean?'

Kate wanted to say no. She didn't know what she was supposed to be looking at. All she saw were hundreds of shoppers wandering in and out of stores. She nodded her head, then thought Alison would need to hear the word. 'Yes,' she said.

'You did this Kate. You and your idea. The number of shoppers has more than doubled since the social media campaign. That's all down to you!'

'Really?' A warm feeling of accomplishment spread around her body. A contented smile brightened her face.

'Yes.' His eyes darkened. If Kate wasn't mistaken, there was an amorousness about his expression. He coughed. It broke the mood. 'Kate, I'd like to invite you out this evening to dinner to celebrate. Would…'

Kate squirmed with inquietude. She would love to go out with him, but she'd agreed to meet her blind date that evening. If she backed out of that, her mother would never let her hear the end of it. Also, Alison might see it as breaking their deal.

'Ivan,' she said, stopping him before he could form the question. 'I'd love to, but tonight I have other plans that I can't get out of.' She gave a nervous laugh. 'My mother has set me up on a blind date. I have to go with my parents to meet their friends' son. He's the blind date.'

She saw his face alter. 'I don't want to go, but there's a reason I have to do it. I can't get into that now. We're going to "The Duchess" restaurant. Have you heard of it?' She knew she was waffling but couldn't seem to keep her mouth closed. 'It's a new place. I don't know what type of food they serve or anything. But I'll have to go. I'm dreading it, to be honest. What about the following day? I could have dinner with you then.' She surprised herself with her forwardness. This aura of certitude she had discovered boosted her confidence. She stared into his big brown eyes, hoping for a positive response.

For a moment, he seemed reticent to agree. He wondered if he'd left his proposal of a date too late. What if she met this unknown guy on the blind date and fell head over heels in love with him? He couldn't let that happen!

He nodded. 'Tomorrow it is, then.'

'Great!' she said and flashed him her biggest smile. Ivan returned it. His hopes had plummeted when she refused. It had taken all his willpower to ask her out. Since losing his wife, he hadn't dated anyone. He felt so out of practice. It had almost crippled him to ask the bright young woman in front of him if she'd accompany him to a restaurant. He still couldn't explain what made her so special, but there was something about her that brought him alive again. She was so animated and full of life; she had lit a spark in him that had long since died. He needed to act now.

Kate searched his eyes and thought she witnessed pain. 'I'd better get to work,' she said.

'I suppose so,' he replied, but he held onto her shoulders, not wanting her to go. Afraid to lose her, and risking everything, he leaned in. His lips lightly kissed hers. 'I shouldn't say this. But I hope your blind date doesn't work out. I want you for myself.'

Kate couldn't answer. Shocked by the kiss, but in a good way, she was lost for words.

'I guess if I don't see you sooner, I'll see you tomorrow for the interview with Tom Brenner.'

Kate hardly dared to breathe. She could explode with happiness. The feel of his lips on hers burned into her memory. His kiss had silenced her words and sent her mind racing with possibilities. Her fingers went to her lips as if she wanted to trap his kiss inside. She dared herself to look into his brooding eyes. 'That sounds great!' she replied.

*

'Well, look who's bothered to show up,' Gary's sarcasm was clear in his tone. 'Has the teacher's pet let you out to play?'

'Yes,' Kate replied, imagining her sister laughing at her discomfort. She frowned, determined to belittle him. 'What teacher? What are you talking about?'

Gary looked momentarily stumped. 'Okay. I mean, the manager's little pet.'

Kate emitted a frustrated sigh. 'Gary, why don't you get a life and keep your nose out of mine?'

Gemma gasped, nudged Mary, and they both giggled.

'Ooh! Trouble in paradise!' Gemma sang maliciously.

Kate ignored her.

'Gemma, stay out of this!' Gary snapped.

'Stay out of what? This is a public area. If you want to have a private conversation, then take it elsewhere!'

'I'm going to get changed,' Kate said, leaving them to their tiff.

Carol followed her out. 'I've seen the toy collection campaign on the internet,' she said, attempting to change the subject and help Kate calm down. 'That was a great idea, Kate. Well done.'

'Thank you,' Kate replied. 'I had no idea it would grow into something so enormous.'

'That's the power of social media these days. It can make or break a person.'

'Ivan and I have been asked to be on Tom Brenner's chat show. Can you believe it?'

Carol gasped and clapped her hands to her mouth. 'Kate, that's fantastic! Ooh, I wish I could go too. Tom Brenner's always been a bit of a heartthrob of mine. He reminds me a lot of Tom Selleck.'

'Who?'

'He was in a series called Magnum P. I. In the eighties, I think it was. He had muscles in all the right places, steely hair and a thick moustache, just like Tom Brenner. Odd they are both named Tom...' she wandered over to her locker and pulled out her pixie costume.

'I guess I could ask Ivan, er, I mean Mr Daniels, if you could come with us,' Kate said. 'I'd like that. You would give me moral support.'

Carol gave her a wan smile. 'Kate, that's a lovely, kind thought, but please don't bother. I can just imagine the mess the grotto would be in if Gary, Gemma, and Mary were there on their own. Those three reprobates would probably have a major fight in the grotto and destroy everything. No. I'll have to stay here.' She paused and took Kate's hands in hers. 'Anyway, I get the impression Ivan would prefer to have you all to himself.'

Kate blushed. 'Do you think so?'

'I do. The way he looked at you when the photographer took those photographs the other day, I'd say he's got it bad.'

'He's asked me out on a date tomorrow night.' She couldn't bring herself to admit to the kiss. She wanted to savour that for herself a little longer.

Carol smiled. 'You go for it, girl. But please, don't break his heart. It's taken him a long time to put himself back out there.'

'I'll look after him,' Kate said, giving Carol a lovesick smile.

Gary and the girls sauntered in to change their clothes. The tension was palpable.

Gemma's eyes glistened with excitement. She hoped Gary would argue again with Kate. The sooner that happened, the sooner Gary would come crawling back to Pixie Pumpernickel and she'd be there, waiting.

Nothing happened between the squabbling Christmas crew until they were in the grotto.

Gemma was at the entrance having her photo taken with more teenage boys and young men than the little kids waiting in line.

Gary had seen her pocket three telephone numbers already, and she'd only been there five minutes. His annoyance was rising. He was losing Kate and now Gemma was flirting with anything in trousers.

He strode over to Kate. 'I saw you.'

Kate scowled. 'You saw what?'

'You, kissing Ivan the Terrible in his office.'

A blush coloured her cheeks. 'That's where you're wrong. He kissed me.'

'Same difference.'

'No, it isn't. Not that it's got anything to do with you!'

'What was his chat up line?'

'Gary! Mind your own business!'

His voice rose in anger. 'Ha! I bet he said, "*Ivan*" enormous penis! Ha ha! Or, no, wait. "*Ivan*" erection with your name on it!'

Kate's eyes narrowed. 'Grow up, Gary!'

Carol scurried over toward them. 'I don't know what's going on here and I don't care. Both of you get back to work and leave your private lives for your free time!'

Brian called Kate into the gingerbread house. She was glad of the respite. Although it wouldn't last long. The next child was heading toward the entrance.

'Kate, I couldn't help but overhear your conversation with Gary. Just ignore him. He's jealous. He knows he doesn't stand a chance next to Ivan. And you know that, too. From what I've seen, Ivan is a good man, and I feel that's exactly what you need. Not some fly-by-night who's out for a good time.'

Kate felt tears pricking the backs of her eyes. How did this man, who hardly knew her, have the intuition to assess her so perfectly?

'Ho, ho, ho! Come here, little boy. Tell Santa what you want for Christmas.'

Kate swiped at her eyes and turned on a smile. She took the child's hand. 'Hi! I'm Pixie Peppercorn. Come with me. I'll take you to see Santa.' The boy pulled on her hand. 'Stop. You've been crying! I bet Father Christmas put you on his naughty list! You naughty pixie!'

'Quite the opposite,' Kate replied, glancing at Brian. 'Santa has given me the best present ever.'

'Yeah? What did you get?'

'The assurance I needed.'

'What's that? A new game for your X-box?'

'Yes,' she replied. 'Something like that.'

'Ho, ho, ho!' Santa chuckled.

Chapter Six

An Unwanted Blind Date.

Kate sat in her bedroom, staring at her image in the dressing-table mirror. She had curled her hair to her shoulders and wore a light covering of make-up. Alison had helped her choose a black evening dress that fell below the knees, and her high-heeled shoes were out on the carpet waiting for her. She was ready to go out on her mother's contrived blind date, but she had zero enthusiasm to attend. Ever since Ivan's kiss she could think of nothing else.

Dorothy shouted up the stairs. 'Kate, are you ready? We're meeting them in twenty minutes.'

'Yes!' she yelled with frustration. Forcing herself off the chair, Kate pushed her feet into the shoes, grabbed her clutch bag and a heavy fur-lined coat and trudged down the stairs. Each step she took dragged her enthusiasm further down with it. Every part of her wanted to call the date off, but she couldn't. If she did, whenever Alison caught up with the recordings, she would find out. Kate would be stuck forever in her parent's home with no plan for the future and no way of escape.

'Awh,' her mother smiled. 'You look lovely, Kate. A little pale, though. Maybe you should put a bit more blusher on those cheeks.'

'I'm fine,' Kate replied. 'Let's get this over with.'

Dorothy sniffed. 'If you go with that attitude, you'll get nowhere.' Kate kept her lips firmly closed.

Conversation in the car was stilted. Every mile closer to the restaurant they got, the more nervous and irritable Kate became.

'This was a bad idea, Mum. I don't think I can go through with it.'

Dorothy turned in her seat and patted her daughter's hand. 'Of course, you can. You're nervous, that's all. Alison said you might feel like this. She told me to tell you she'd be with you every step of the way.' Dorothy sniffed. 'I don't see how, when she's out on a case this evening, but what do I know?'

Kate fumed. Knowing Alison was listening in and probably having a good laugh at her expense annoyed her even more. 'Alright! Come on. Let's get this over with!'

After Alan found a parking space, they picked their way through lightly fallen snow to the restaurant. Kate pulled her coat tighter around her. The biting cold wind wrestled with her beautifully coiffured hair and whipped it across her face until she resembled a scraggly scarecrow. *Some first impression I'm going to make!* She thought.

Inside, Alan gave their name to the snooty maitre d'.

'Ah, yes, sir. Your guests are waiting for you,' he sniffed.

They followed him in a line, like a gaggle of goslings following their mother, through the heart of the restaurant. Kate dawdled, bringing up the rear. She noticed the subdued lighting with its pink hue. Heavy tablecloths covered every table and almost reached the floor. Two huge chandeliers hung from the ceilings, and thick velvet curtains in a dark chocolate brown hung at the windows. Low chamber music echoed around them as though they had stepped back in time to a simpler age and smells of spices and cooked meats radiated around her.

Kate pasted on a smile when they reached their allocated table. Her parents spoke to their friends, but when they moved aside to introduce her, her faint smile slipped to the floor quicker than a pedestrian on an icy street.

'YOU!' malice dripped from her one exaggerated word. The four adults gasped.

Civil Servant, Mike, sat at the table. He looked as shocked as she was.

'MOTHER! What have you done? Why didn't you tell me her name? Then I could have saved us all from this fiasco.'

Dorothy grabbed Kate's arm and pulled her into her seat. 'Kate, sit down. Now, both of you calm down. I don't know what's going on here but do not make a scene. I'll never live it down if we get thrown out of this restaurant.'

Mike's mother nodded. 'You too Michael. Act your age, not your shoe size.'

Mike rolled his eyes and stabbed the heel of his fork into the tabletop. 'How many times do I have to tell you? That saying went out with the ark! And my name's Mike, not Michael. I'm not six years old anymore, mother!'

Kate sniffed. 'Then stop acting like it.' She turned to her parents. 'Mum, Dad, this is the guy who said the only possible job he could get me was as a pixie in a grotto. He did it out of spite because I wouldn't go to the stupid school dance with him years ago.'

Dorothy smiled at her daughter and nodded. 'Then you should thank him.'

Kate gawped at her mother as if she'd suddenly transformed into the ghost of Christmas past. 'What are you saying? Why?'

'Because you've got your photo in the local paper, for creating such a great campaign for underprivileged children. That's a great accolade, Kate.'

Alan joined in. He reached across the table and shook Mike's hand. 'It's true, Mike. Thanks to you, she's also going to be in a national newspaper. And this weekend, she'll appear on the Tom Brenner Chat show with Mr Daniels, the manager of Silver Springs Shopping Centre. So, we really couldn't thank you enough, Mike. If you hadn't given her the job, she'd probably be still sitting at home feeling sorry for herself.'

'Dad!' Kate snapped.

'He's only telling the truth, Kate,' Dorothy intervened. 'Your success is all down to Mike here. So, I think the least you can both do is sit and have a meal together.'

Livid. Mike's face burned red with annoyance. He had wanted to belittle her, not make her into an overnight sensation. His plan had seriously backfired. He couldn't believe it!

Kate didn't want to stay there but felt forced to sit opposite him. The way her dad had told Mike about her success had been perfect. Alan had such an innocence about him that nobody could accuse him of bragging.

'Yeah, thanks Mike,' Kate said, realising her dad had a point. 'And I apologise for not going to the dance with you years ago. There, I've said it. Can you just forget it now?' She flashed him a false smile. She knew her final remark was acerbic and twisted. That was what she wanted. His parents would think she was trying her best, but Mike would know she had won and his pathetic attempt at revenge had backfired.

Mike wanted to hit out at something. His plan to degrade her had exploded in his face. Not going to the school dance may have been nothing to her, but he would never forget it. He'd worked up the courage to ask her. He'd even told all his mates he was going to do it. They'd watched him head over to her. They'd seen her scowl then shake her head, and they'd laughed at him for weeks afterwards. It was all her fault. His hands balled into fists under the table. He would have to retreat and plan something else to get his revenge on Kate Massey.

After the desserts, Kate excused herself to use the restrooms. She needed a break. Mike's hatred tainted everything. It stretched outwards like gamma rays burning into her soul.

As she neared the back of the restaurant, she stepped back in shock.

'Ivan! What are you doing here?'

The general manager had the decency to look embarrassed. 'Kate, sorry. I'm ashamed to admit, I came to see who I was up against.'

'I don't understand.'

'You said you were going on a blind date. I wanted to see who my competition was.'

When Kate burst into laughter and tapped him on his shoulder, his anxiety melted away.

'Ha! Don't be silly. It's a guy who used to go to the same school as me. Don't worry. He hates me. I wouldn't go to the school dance with him, and he's taken umbrage ever since.'

'Why don't you sit down and have a drink with me? You can get a break from him, then.'

Kate's eyes sparkled with devilment. 'Yeah, that would be great, but I've got a better idea. Why don't you come to our table? That will really annoy him. Ooh! If I say you're my boyfriend, that'll stick the knife in even further!'

Ivan bit his lip. 'No. It's better to say I'm your boss. Otherwise, it would seem odd that you'd agree to a blind date.'

'Good point. I'll nip to the loo and then I'll introduce you to everyone.'

'Mum, Dad, Mr and Mrs Abbott, Mike, this is Ivan Daniels. He's my manager at the shopping centre. He was sitting at the bar having a drink. I've invited him to join us. I hope nobody minds.'

Her thoughts drifted to her sister. She hoped Alison was enjoying all this. It would show her how much her little sis was evolving and becoming her own stronger person.

Alan stood up. 'Hello Ivan, I'm Alan, Kate's father. It's so nice to meet you. Kate has told us all about you. We are so happy she's fitting in so well at Silver Springs.'

Ivan gripped both of Alan's hands in his. 'Believe me, Alan, she is a real asset to the team.'

'Excellent. That's great to hear. You have Mike here to thank for that. He gave her the information to apply for the job.'

Ivan reached out to shake Mike's hand.

Mike forced himself to take it and faked a smile. He didn't mention he had spoken to Ivan on the phone when he'd fabricated the story of Kate crooning on cruise ships.

'She's got a real head for business has Kate,' Ivan said, singing her praises.

Kate grinned. The four parents nodded and smiled, while Mike contemplated his coffee cup. He wished it was big enough to drown himself in.

Chapter Seven

A Television Sensation

December 13th

Kate woke to the sound of Christmas carols coming from her father's old stereo in the living room and him singing along with them. 'We three kings if Orient are... dah de dah de dah de dah.'

She smiled and stretched, remembering her evening out the night before. What had started out as a disaster had turned into something exciting. She hadn't believed it when Ivan had appeared. He said he was checking on his competition. It surprised her he cared that much.

Later, when she asked him to join them, he sat next to her. Under the table, his hand landed on her knee, squeezed it and stayed there. She had felt tingly all over and couldn't remove the huge grin that refused to leave her happy face.

Kate giggled, remembering their departure from the restaurant. Mrs Abbott had asked her and Mike if they wanted to see each other again.

'No way!' Mike had snapped.

But Kate was obliged to answer positively.

'Yeah, I'll see your son again... when he changes his attitude or when hell freezes over. Whatever happens first.'

At that moment, she couldn't care less if Alison disallowed it. She was livid. She'd had to spend the night looking at his maudlin features and she couldn't do it any longer.

Mr and Mrs Abbott had gasped. Mike glowered, and Ivan burst

into laughter.

Dorothy scowled. 'Kate that was uncalled for.'

'Maybe, but it's true.'

Alan defended his daughter. 'I'm sorry, but I agree, Dorothy. At least Kate has tried to be civil this evening.'

'Yeah, and considering he's a civil servant, he's not exactly living up to expectation, is he?' Kate replied.

Ivan laughed again. He tried to convert it into a cough but didn't quite succeed.

'KATE! Breakfast!' Alan shouted up the stairs, dragging her back to the present.

Today was her television appearance on Tom Brenner's chat show. She felt petrified about appearing on live television, yet knowing she'd get to spend the whole day with Ivan sent tingles of excitement up and down her spine.

In the kitchen, she gobbled down her breakfast while half listening to her mother reliving the previous evening. '...I mean, I hope it won't affect my friendship with Mike's mother. That's the only thing worrying me.'

'It'll be fine, Mum. She must know by now her son's a miserable, grudge-holding loser.'

Dorothy paused. She wanted to reprehend her daughter but couldn't. Kate only spoke the truth. It wasn't normal to hold on to a vendetta for so many years. At least she didn't think it was. Keeping something inside like that only festered and became cancerous. And when

Kate had apologised to him last night, to clear the air, he hadn't even said thank you. 'I guess you're right,' she replied.

Alan came strolling into the kitchen with Sunday bounding at his heels.

'Where have you been, Alan?' Dorothy flicked a tea towel in his direction and muttered under her breath. 'The coffee I made you went cold half an hour ago. You said you were going for a paper. That doesn't take an hour and a half.'

'Sorry!' He rolled his eyes at Kate when Dorothy turned back to the stove. 'I saw an old friend. We got chatting. As you do. Anyway, I had a good catch up with him, and Sunday had a nice long walk. So, all is well with the world, on this "cold and frosty morning."' He sang the last four words.

Kate grinned. Dorothy didn't.

Half a mile away, Mike dropped a bag of steaming dog poop on the angry neighbour's lawn. He threw the plastic bag into the nearest garden, then approached the old man's door.

'Hi, sorry to bother you. You may remember I was witness to the young woman and her dog who did its business on the verge outside your house.'

'Oh, yes, I remember. What can I do for you?'

'I've just had words with her. I'm afraid to say her dog has done it again.'

The old man's eyes narrowed. 'You're joking!'

'I wish I was. Only, this time it's worse! She let it enter your garden. It's pooped on your beautiful lawn. I told her to clean it up. She told me to go forth and multiply.'

The old man scowled. 'What do you mean?'

'She told me to go away by using the F word.'

The neighbour gasped. 'How rude!'

'I know, right? Some people have no scruples. You would have thought that, as she's been in the local paper, she'd be more accommodating, wouldn't you?'

'What are you talking about?'

'She's the young woman working in Silver Springs Shopping Centre.'

'Do you mean the girl who's organised the used toy collection?'

'That's the one.'

'Unbelievable! I might have to pay a visit to the grotto and have words with the little nuisance. It's about time people found out what she's really like.'

'My thoughts exactly! Would you like me to help you clean up the mess?' Mike crossed his fingers behind his back.

'No, there's no need. Thank you for letting me know.'

'It was my pleasure,' Mike smiled.

*

Gary cuddled up to Gemma on the staffroom couch and whispered in her ear. He had reluctantly agreed to go out with her the night before, but now he was glad he did. He could make Kate jealous by acting amorously in front of her.

Unfortunately, Kate didn't give them a second glance. She waved to Carol who stood at the kitchen counters making tea as usual, then went straight through to the changing room.

Gemma turned to Gary, who had frozen to the spot. He watched Kate's exit with a hint of annoyance. She hadn't even glimpsed in their direction!

Gemma's exaggerated giggling had also been for Kate's benefit, but it hadn't attained the required effect.

Oblivious to Gary and Gemma's games, Kate slipped into her costume and applied her make-up. Pulling on her thick winter coat and outdoor boots, she threw her pixie hat and boots in a holdall and headed to Ivan's office.

He must have seen her coming because he stood at the open door, waiting for her.   His face broke into a grin. 'Let's go, Pixie Peppercorn and future star of television?'

'Ha! Future tongue-tied loser, you mean. I'm dreading it!'
'You'll be fine. I'll be there with you for moral support.'
'Thank goodness for that!'
'But I'll be just as nervous.'
'Ivan!' she tapped his forearm and sulked. 'That's not helping me at all!'

'I know, but it's true. I'm used to sitting in my office behind a closed door. Any visitors I speak to, I deal with them from behind my enormous desk. It acts like my shield, protecting me from anyone getting too close. But today, we'll be sitting on huge comfy sofas in full view of a live audience and heaven knows how many other viewers at home.'   'Ivan. Please, shut up! You're not helping me in the slightest!' She saw his shoulders slump. 'Come on. Let's go,' she said. 'The sooner we get this over with, the better!'

*

Kate and Ivan mingled in the Green Room with the other guests who were also appearing on the Tom Brenner chat show. Kate picked at a sandwich while Ivan clutched his flute of champagne and constantly tapped his heel on the floor with nervous tension.

'Stop it!' Kate batted his leg with her free hand. 'You're making me even more nervous by doing that!'

'Sorry.' His mouth sunk at the corners and his puppy dog eyes made her heart melt quicker than a hanging icicle.

'We'll be fine. If we stick together, we can do this!' She hoped her words sounded more assertive than she felt. Her spittle was almost non-existent, and her stomach was performing somersaults.

Ivan wrapped her in his arms and kissed her forehead. 'You might be little in stature, but you're huge in strength and determination.'

Kate revelled in his embrace. She felt at home but was unsure where their relationship, if you could even call it that, was heading. It worried her. What if he didn't have genuine feelings for her? Was this just a Christmas fling because he didn't want to be alone?

What are you worried about? Her conscience asked. *Didn't you say you wanted exactly that? A Christmas fling to get over your ex?* She answered in the affirmative despite talking to herself. *So, just go with it. Whatever happens, happens.*

'Kate Massey and Ivan Daniels?'

Hearing her name stopped her daydreaming.

Ivan jumped away from her as if she'd electrocuted him. 'Yeah. That's us.'

'Great. I'm Adam. And I'll be taking you to the set.' He scowled at Ivan. 'Here, put this on.' The flustered young organiser thrust a Santa hat into Ivan's hand. 'Then you'll look more in the Christmas spirit. Less like a shopping centre manager and more… how can I put this? More natural.'

Kate giggled.

Ivan snatched the hat, rammed it on his head, and frowned at the man. 'Fine!'

Kate reached up and repositioned it. Her kind smile eased his nerves. 'There, that's better. You look handsome. All the women will fall in love with you.'

'I only need you to do that,' he said with a sad smile.

Kate's heart skipped a beat. She felt a reddening blush creeping up her neck. 'Ivan, I... er...'

'Come on, guys. Chop, chop!' Adam ushered them out of the green room. 'You're on in two minutes.'

'Two minutes?' Kate mouthed.

Ivan grasped hold of her hand and squeezed as they strode toward the set.

'... And now, I'd like to introduce two members of Silver Springs Shopping Centre, Ha! It almost sounds like a tongue twister, doesn't it? Anyway, please give a warm welcome to Kate Massey and Ivan Daniels.'

They walked on set to rapturous applause, both oblivious they were still holding hands. Each other's touch eased their escalating nerves.

'Now, this is a great little story,' Tom began. 'Ivan, here, who is the manager of the entire shopping centre was looking for ways to attract more customers to shop at the centre, and I believe it was Kate who came up with the idea for the used toys collection. Is that correct, Ivan?'

'Yes,' he said, clearing his throat and sitting up straight.

'So, Kate, how did you come up with the idea?'

'To be honest, I thought about Christmases at home when I was a kid. Every year, my mum would ask my sister and me to tidy up our toys to make room for the new ones. What we no longer played with, mum either gave them to younger family members, you know, cousins etcetera, or we donated them to charity. I thought that most parents probably did something similar. Then I thought if they could encourage their kids to give their used toys to Santa, perhaps they wouldn't feel too bad giving them away.'

'That's a great idea!' Tom replied. 'And Ivan, why do you think Kate's idea took off so quickly and successfully?'

'Well, Tom,' Ivan said. He crossed his legs and leaned back on the sofa, relaxing and enjoying the experience. 'I believe it's all down to Kate and her exuberance for life...'

*

Back in the green room, Kate and Ivan drank more champagne. They couldn't stop grinning. The interview had been a great success. Tom had put them both at ease, and Ivan had forgotten all about the audience and viewers. He spoke to Tom as though they were at home in his living room, not in front of a live audience, and whatever he said would be broadcast on a television set and watched by millions of people.

'You were great, Kate, but you realise with all this publicity and now the television coverage we will be even more inundated with shoppers and used toys, don't you?'

'Yes, but that's what we want, isn't it? The more people come, the more money the centre will make. That's the whole point, isn't it?'

Ivan grinned. He loved the way she referred to everything by using the collective "we". He dared to hope their budding relationship would flourish into a love affair that surpassed any other.

'It sure is. Kate! I just don't think you realise what you've done. This will put the shopping centre way up in the overall rankings. I could be in for an extra-large bonus and that's all down to you, Pixie Peppercorn.'

'Great!' she answered with a grin. 'I suppose the least you could do is take me out to dinner when you get that enormous amount of money.' Kate gasped. She couldn't believe she'd said that! She swore it was all down to Alison listening in. She wanted to shock her detective sister and show her how much she was breaking out of her shell.

'Consider it done,' he grinned. 'But in the meantime, stop eating those curled-up sandwiches. I'm taking you out for a proper lunch.' He reached for her hand and gently squeezed.

A flush of oxytocin coursed through her body, awakening her sexual desire from the top of her head to the tips of her toes. Kate wanted so much to kiss him there and then, but she held back.

'Sounds good to me,' she said, flashing him her dazzling smile, that made him feel warm all over.

*

'And what time do you call this!' Alison said from the sofa as her sister fussed over the dog and wandered inside.

Kate flushed. 'It's only midnight.'

'Only, she says! You've had Mum and Dad wandering around like caged animals waiting to congratulate you on your premier television performance. Where've you been?'

'Out with Ivan. Weren't you listening in to the conversation?'

'Kate, I've been working on a case all day. The last thing I wanted to do was listen in to my little sister getting it on with Ivan the Great.'

Kate giggled. All the champagne and wine she'd drunk had kept her in a happy, tipsy, mood all day. 'That's better than what Gary called him.'

'Why? What did that idiot say?'

'He called him *"Ivan* an enormous penis."'

Alison burst into laughter. 'And has he?'

'Alison, if I have to answer yes, I will, but it would be a lie.'

'Uff! I'll let that one slide. So, I'm guessing he hasn't then?'

'Hasn't what?'

'Got an enormous thingummy.'

'I don't know. Things haven't got that far. If you'd listened to the recordings, you'd know! We've only kissed.'

Alison grinned. 'That's a start. Did you like it?'

Kate's eyes clouded over. 'Yes, of course I did.'

'I'm going to assume you're not just saying that because of our deal.' Alison's eyes squinted toward her sister, looking for verification.

'Yes, that's correct.'

'Alright, so sit down and tell me all about your day.' She paused. 'I tell you what. For the moment, the bet doesn't count. You can talk freely to me.'

'Great!' Kate slumped into her favourite armchair and told her sister all about it.

Chapter Eight

Gotcha!

December 14th

Kate awoke to her father shouting up the stairs.

'Kate, there's a gentleman here who would like to talk to you.'

Her heart skipped a beat. *It must be Ivan. He can't wait to see me again.* She jumped out of bed, headed for the mirror, and scowled at her reflection.

'Give me five minutes!' she shouted.

In a frantic race to make herself look presentable, she ran to the bathroom, washed her face, brushed her teeth, and raced back into the bedroom. She threw on a shirt and jeans, dragged a brush through her matted hair, slipped on some flat pumps and galloped down the staircase, pinching her cheeks to give herself a bit of colour.

The huge smile on her face soon disappeared when she discovered who was standing on the doorstep.

'Huh! There she is. The woman who lets her dog foul the pavements every single day. And has now progressed to my lawn!'

Kate stood open-mouthed. The neighbour who had confronted her a few days ago stood on the welcome mat, his hands balled into fists and a suspicious-looking carrier bag hung over one arm.

'How did you know where I lived?' she thought aloud.

The neighbour squirmed on the spot. 'A little bird told me.' 'A little turd, more like!' Kate replied, her thoughts springing straight to Mike.

A frown crossed his face. 'Speaking of which; I demand to know what you intend to do about your dog! It's progressed from doing its business all over the streets to now leaving its poo in my garden!' He pointed an accusatory finger in Kate's face. 'And I believe you've taught it to do that!'

'Now, wait just a minute!' Alan butted in. 'I don't know what's going on here, but you can't come to my house and attack my daughter on the doorstep.'

'Her dog is fouling the paths and people's gardens every day, and she never even attempts to pick it up.' He waggled the plastic bag as proof. 'That's not true!' Kate replied. 'I told you the other evening, that it wasn't my dog that left the mess outside your home.'

'But you would say that. You're hardly likely to tell me the truth, are you?'

'YES, I am!' Kate replied.

Alan stepped in. 'I honestly think you've made a mistake here. My daughter has been so busy at work that the dog-walking duties have fallen on my shoulders. She hasn't walked Sunday for the last few days. I think you may be barking up the wrong tree.' He grinned at the doggy idiom.

Lost for words. The angry neighbour curled his hands into fists, the handles of the plastic bag crinkling in protest. 'You would say that though, wouldn't you?' He scowled at Alan. 'You're bound to defend her, aren't you?'

Affronted, Alan could only muster, 'Well, I never…'

The neighbour turned to Kate. His eyes narrowed. 'You might have your father there to back you up, but you haven't heard the end of this.' He threw the plastic bag in the garden, then stomped down the driveway, his breath billowing out in icy waves of angry mist.

'Huh! The nerve of the man!' Alan sniffed. 'As if either of us wouldn't pick up after the dog!'

Kate nodded, lost for words. Somehow, she didn't think she'd seen the end of her angry neighbour and she felt certain Mike was behind it.

That afternoon, she wandered into work, unaware that she had become an overnight sensation. Dressed in her mother's ugly big coat, capacious boots, a thick red scarf around her neck and matching gloves, she gazed in amazement when shop owners and customers clapped her as she wandered past. Two people even asked for her autograph, which took her completely by surprise.

She was relieved to reach the staff room, but even there, she met a packed room full of staff members who patted her on the back and congratulated her.

'Thanks,' she muttered. *What was the big deal? Okay, she'd appeared on television, but that hardly made her a star.*

Gary strutted over to her. 'You've no idea what's going on, have you?'

'Yes?' she said, wishing she could tell the truth and dying a little inside.

'Oh Yeah? Then tell me.'

Kate shrugged. 'Alright, I think you'd better explain.'

'After your TV appearance, the number of customers has quadrupled. We've got more second-hand toys than we know what to do with and we've had to hire more staff in the food court to keep up with demand. You are everyone's best friend!'

Gemma squirmed on the sofa and crossed her arms and legs. 'Huh! Not everyone's!' she sniffed.

'Lots of people will get better Christmas bonuses because of the number of sales they are making. Everyone is on a high, and that's all down to you.'

'Well, Iva... Mr Daniels too,' Kate said, not wanting to bask in all the glory.

'He helped,' Carol said, stirring a cup of tea. 'But you are the face of Silver Springs.'

Kate blushed. 'Yeah, right! As if!'

'It's true!' Gary confirmed.

'Speaking of which,' Carol said. 'We'd better get a move on. According to the security staff, the line of kids waiting to hand in their old toys and see Father Christmas has an hour's waiting time already.'

When Kate headed to the grotto, she couldn't believe what she was witnessing. A pile of toys over eight feet tall towered over her. Two maintenance men were putting the donations into hessian sacks to take them into the bowels of the shopping centre. Kate hoped they'd move a little faster. She felt sure if health and safety turned up, they would consider the toy mountain a fire hazard.

'There she is!' she heard a father shout. 'That's Pixie Peppercorn!'

The patter of hundreds of tiny feet running on the shiny tiles reminded Kate of a sudden rainstorm. Inundated by tiny hands shoving autograph books in front of her face, hugging her and a hundred voices all shouting to be heard was overwhelming. She smiled and scribbled, laughed and joked, trying to appease each tiny human.

The chaos only subsided when Brian appeared in the gingerbread doorway dressed as Santa.

'Ho, ho, ho! What is all this noise? Are you attacking Pixie Peppercorn?'

'NO!' they shouted.

'I should think not! I don't want to add any more names to my naughty list. Now. Everyone. Make an orderly line and I'll see each one of you in a moment.'

The children, overwhelmed from speaking and seeing the big man himself, shuffled back to their parents, who had no intention of losing their position in the ever-lengthening queue.

Kate breathed a sigh of relief. She was about to take her place in the grotto when she heard Ivan calling her name.

He grinned when her face erupted in a huge smile.

'Hi, Pixie Peppercorn! How are you?'

'I'm fine, thanks. You?'

'Great. I was wondering if you'd like to go out tomorrow night. My niece is in the local pantomime. I promised to go, but don't want to be a "Bill-no-mates" and turn up alone. So, I thought I'd ask you.'

Kate laughed. 'That's not the best way to ask someone out! I feel you're asking just so you're not alone!'

Ivan's smile disappeared. 'Kate, please, don't ever think that. I enjoy your company.'

Kate tapped his forearm. 'I'm playing with you, Ivan. Of course, I'd love to go to the pantomime with you.' *I'd go anywhere with you!* She thought.

His smile reappeared. 'Great. I'll pick you up at six-thirty, alright?'

Carol ran over, disrupting the burning sexual tension building between them. 'Sorry to interrupt, Mr Daniels, but I need Kate to return to her grotto duties. Several children are demanding autographs.'

Kate giggled. 'This is getting out of control. I'm a nobody. Why would anyone want my signature?'

Carol looked embarrassed. 'It's Pixie Peppercorn's autograph they're asking for.'

Kate blushed. 'Oh. Yes, of course. How silly of me.'

'Yes, Carol, take her back to work, please,' Ivan replied, giving Kate a sly wink.

Carol saw it but pretended she didn't. A long time had passed since she had seen her boss smile. She hoped Kate would stay for a while.

*

December 15th

Kate woke to the sound of metal clanking on metal. She recognised the comforting sound. It was a cake tin hitting the oven rails.

Seconds later, her mother turned up the volume on her Michael Bublé Christmas album on the ancient stereo system in the living room and shouted to Alan.

'Don't disappear for two hours with Sunday, like you usually do. We've got a mountain of things to do this morning.'

'I'll be as quick as I can. What's the hurry?'

'We're helping Kate with the WI Bake sale in the shopping centre, remember?'

'Oh, yes, of course. We won't be long.'

Kate heard the front door close and Sunday's distinctive bark as he set off on his walk. Kate knew she had neglected her dog since her arrival back home. First, because she was so depressed and second, because her social life had taken off. She couldn't remember the last time she'd given her ex-boyfriend a second thought, and that was a great feeling!

There were only two flies in the ointment of her life: Mike with his malicious vendetta, and the angry neighbour. She wondered if she should have gone with her dad. That way, they would both have a protector if the guy sprung out from behind a bush and verbally assaulted them. She also wanted to play detective and follow Mike. She couldn't shake the niggling doubt that he continued to feed the neighbour malicious untruths to turn him against her.

Her mother put an end to her musings.

'Kate! Get yourself downstairs right now. I'm going to need your help with all these cakes and buns.'

With a sigh, Kate flung back the covers and headed downstairs.

Dorothy took one look at her daughter and shook her head. 'Oh, no! You're not baking in your pyjamas. Go upstairs, get washed and dressed. Be down here in fifteen minutes. We've got a lot to do.'

Kate flopped into a chair. She held out a hand in a supplicating pose. 'Please! Can you spare a mug of coffee first for a tired, overworked pixie?' Her arm and head dropped dramatically onto the kitchen table. Dorothy rolled her eyes toward the kitchen ceiling. 'Huh!' she said. 'The youth of today has no stamina. In my day, we were up with the cock crow and went to bed when we could no longer see.' 'Yeah, yeah, I know. You trudged to school in snow up to your waist, you had no electricity, the internet didn't exist, and you had to get up to change the few channels on the telly.'

Dorothy flipped a tea towel in her daughter's direction. 'Sarcasm is the lowest form of wit, Kate. Now, hurry! You've got thirteen minutes left to get your backside back down here or I'll ground you for a week.' 'Ground me? Mother, I'm twenty-four years old!'

'Then it's about time you acted like it.' She shoved a mug of coffee in her daughter's hands.

Kate knew not to push her mother any further. Dorothy's laser beam eyes looked like they were about to burn her body to a crisp.

'Yeah, yeah, I'm going,' she said, swiping a piping hot mince pie from a cooling tray.

'Hey!' Dorothy's tea towel flicked in Kate's direction again. 'Get out of here! Stop eating the merchandise!'

Alan appeared almost two hours later when Dorothy and Kate had an extensive selection of cakes, buns and biscuits displayed on the kitchen table, all at various stages of completion.

'Where have you been?' Dorothy snapped, waving the icing bag in his direction.

'I went for a longer walk than usual, Dorothy because I was hoping to bump into that man who came to our house yesterday.'

'Did you find him, Dad?'

'No, Kate, I didn't. But the more I think about it, the more out of order I think he was. What proof does he have that Sunday is making a mess?'

'None. That's what annoys me.'

'Then where's he getting his information from?'

'I think it's Mike. I just can't prove it.'

Dorothy shook her head. 'I can't see it being him. He's got a good job.'

'Mother! Serial killers have jobs. But they still go around murdering people!'

Her mother sniffed. 'Then you need to get some proof, don't you, young lady?'

Kate clicked her tongue, thinking again that her mother talked to her like she was still a kid. 'Yes, Mummy,' she replied, sarcasm dripping from every syllable.

'Stop talking and keep icing those Christmas tree biscuits, or we'll never be ready on time. Alan, when you've dried Sunday's feet, I need you to help me with the fairy cakes.'

'Yes, dear,' he said with a sigh.

*

Kate's workmates stared at the mountain of Tupperware boxes her parents were carrying. They had more cakes and fancies than the entire Women's Institute.

'Wow!' Carol looked at Kate. 'When did you get time to make all this?' She pointed to an empty table where her two cakes and a dozen buns lingered like wallflowers at a school dance. Please, put all your things on here.

'My mum did most of it. She's a great baker.' Kate said, linking her arm through her mother's.

Dorothy beamed from ear to ear. 'Kate helped me a lot. Especially with the icing.'

'Come on, mum. I'll help you set up then I'll have to get changed,' Kate said.

Ivan appeared when Kate had left, and her parents had almost finished.

'Wow! Mr and Mrs Massey, your stall looks amazing! My mouth's watering just looking at it all.'

Dorothy preened. She leaned towards him and whispered, 'Help yourself to a piece of chocolate log, a mince pie, a shortbread biscuit or whatever you fancy. And please, Ivan, call me Dorothy.'

Ivan chose a piece of Christmas cake and bit into it. 'Oh! This is gorgeous, Dorothy!' He replied, his mouth awash with flavours. It's been a while since I've had a piece of Christmas cake. That's delicious!'

'Thank you, Ivan.' Kate had told her he had lost his wife and child a few years ago. She imagined him sitting in the dark at home, wishing Christmas would pass. She came around to the front of the stall and linked her arm through his. 'So, tell me, Ivan. What plans have you got for Christmas?'

Kate supervised the used toy collection and ushered the children towards Santa's gingerbread house.

Gemma and Mary could only look on and seethe. It was so unfair she got all the attention and glory.

Gemma still received wolf whistles from teenage boys and some young men as they passed by, but it wasn't enough. She wanted to be in the newspaper and appear on TV. Life wasn't fair!

Mary knew she had no chance of that happening to her. Carol hid her away at every available opportunity. Today she wore a sweltering snowman costume. It hid her girth but did nothing for her self-esteem. Her face, hidden inside the large furry head, was dripping with sweat. It didn't help her acne one bit!

Their disgruntled heads turned as one when an angry male voice echoed around the shopping centre.

'There she is!' the old man bellowed. 'She's the one!'

Shoppers stopped what they were doing and scanned the shopping centre to find the owner of the scathing vitriol.

Kate groaned. She felt sick. Instinct warned her to conceal herself. All she wanted to do was jump inside the gingerbread house and hide under Santa's throne, yet her legs refused to move. She recognised him immediately. Her outraged neighbour stabbed an accusatory finger in Kate's direction.

'Standing there in the middle of the grotto, looking all innocent, cute and perfect, like butter wouldn't melt. Little miss prim. Well, let me tell you…' he opened his arms and swung around to face his makeshift audience. 'She is anything but. This… this… woman allows her dog to do its business all around the neighbourhood and never picks up after it! How about that?'

More than half of the instant audience walked away, they had been expecting a much juicier story than that. some others remained, with nothing in particular to do, they hung around waiting to see if it got any better. A fist fight with Santa's pixie would be great to plaster all over social media. In anticipation, they fiddled in their pockets and bags searching for their phones.

Gemma and Mary were no better. They huddled together, nudging each other and enjoying every minute of Kate's belittling and cringeworthy situation.

'Sir, as I've told you before, that isn't true. I would never do that!' She glanced around at the interested shoppers and baulked. Leaning by a pillar with his arms and legs crossed, watching the commotion, was Mike. He caught her eye, saluted and smirked.

Anger rose inside her, surging through her veins like bubbling lava. She wanted to have real pixie power, fly across the room, grab him by the throat, hoist him up to the ceiling and wring his scrawny neck! Now she was certain he had instigated the entire event. Hell, he'd most probably driven the irate pension here in his car! This was another attempt at getting even for the school dance. How petty and closed-minded could he be?

Right, you shallow attempt at a human being, she thought. *You will not let this drop, so neither will I. Look out Mike Abbott I'm coming after you!*

The neighbour's tirade of defamation continued as Ivan and four security guards came rushing over.

'This false effort of a human being wants you all to think she is good-hearted and is doing this toy thing for the benefit of those in need, but out of sight of the public eye, she walks her dog and lets it foul pathways. She allows it to leave its mess in people's driveways and then denies she had anything to do with it. Where's her Christmas spirit then? Huh?'

'Kate, go to the staff room,' Ivan ordered., his face set.

As she scurried away, her face burning with embarrassment and Gemma and Mary's laughter following behind her, Gary ran to catch her up.

'Come on,' he said, escorting her away. 'Ignore him. He's out of his mind.'

Ivan turned to the pensioner, trying to keep his own anger under control.

'Sir, what you are saying amounts to slander. Where is your proof? How dare you come into a public place shouting, bellowing and upsetting my staff when you haven't one shred of evidence it's her dog?'

'It's her! It's got to be.' His eyes scanned the crowd. He spied Mike. 'He told me it was her.'

Mike gasped. He slid around the back of the pillar, but not before Ivan saw him.

'Throw both men out of the shopping centre. If they don't go quietly, take them to my office,' Ivan told the guards. 'I may have them arrested. One for slander and the other for disturbing the peace.'

The security men took hold of the old man's arms and dragged him away kicking and shouting at the top of his voice. 'SHE'S A FAKE. A DO-GOODER WHO ISN'T LIVING UP TO HER NAME. PICK UP AFTER YOUR DOG YOU DIRTY, POOR EXAMPLE OF A HUMAN BEING!'

Ivan raced toward the pillar ready for a confrontation.

Alan appeared. He had also heard the commotion and seen the neighbour pointing out Mike. His blood boiled. How could Mike be so petty? And how dare the neighbour humiliate Kate in front of hundreds of shoppers? If this got posted on social media, it would ruin his daughter's reputation. Everything she had achieved would disintegrate in a flash.

He and Ivan approached the pillar from either side, but Mike had disappeared.

'This has got way out of hand.' Alan said. 'He's embarrassed my daughter and I'm not about to accept that.'

'Don't worry, Alan. I'll bring an end to this. I promise.'

Despite his anger, Alan stopped. He studied the man in front of him and his eyes softened. 'Wow! Ivan, you've got it bad, haven't you?'

'I ...'

'You're in love with my daughter!' Alan grabbed him by the biceps and grinned. 'That's perfect! I know she's in good hands with you, Ivan.'

Ivan's face grew serious. 'I'll look after her, Alan, I swear. But first, we have to put a stop to these slanderous allegations.'

Alan nodded. 'Whatever you need, count me in!'

*

In the staff room, Gary passed crying Kate a tissue.

'Here. Wipe your eyes.' He turned on the kettle and popped a teabag into a semi-clean mug. 'That was intense! What's going on?'

Through sniffles, Kate explained the whole situation.

Gary finished the tea and brought it over to her. 'That Mike guy doesn't sound right in the head. So, he got stood up at the high school dance. So what? That was years ago. I mean, come on, man, move on.'

Gary's choice of words made her laugh.

'Exactly.' She leaned her head onto his shoulder, craving a bit of comfort. 'Thank you for your support.'

It was the wrong thing to do.

Gary misread her signals. He pulled her into his arms. Instinctively, he kissed the top of her head… just as Ivan walked into the room.

'Oh!' Ivan appeared frozen to the spot. 'Sorry. I, er….' He turned on his heels and fled.

'Ivan, wait!' Kate yelled.

Gary pulled away. A building feeling of glee warmed his stomach. He'd seen Ivan's face. His boss couldn't comprehend what he had witnessed. Now he would see Kate in a different light. Maybe she wasn't the one-man woman Ivan was searching for.

'Leave it, Kate. Speak to him after work when he's calmed down,' he said, hoping his suggestion was good enough to convince Kate he cared.   Carol raced into the staff room. 'I need you both back in the grotto right now!' She ran a frazzled hand through her untidy hair.

'Gemma and Mary can't cope.'

'Huh! Nothing new there then,' Gary's sarcastic comment hung around the staffroom as he sauntered away.

Kate replayed and replayed the last few seconds of her life and wanted to scream. What had possessed her to put her head on Gary's shoulder? She should have known he would take that as an invitation to make a move on her. A groan escaped her lips when she relived the look of horror and disappointment on Ivan's face. Kate gripped the edge of the sofa cushion, wishing she could turn back the clock. Everything had been going so well and now she was certain she'd blown it. The expression of hurt and disillusionment Ivan had portrayed left her in no doubt about how much she had devastated him. She had opened a fresh wound next to the scars he already carried.

'Kate, come on. Please!' Carol's insistence forced Kate to stand up and follow her outside.

Kate had only been back in the grotto for a few minutes when Ivan appeared. His thin lips set in a hard line displayed his emotions. His eyes refused to look at her.

'Kate, there is another newspaper here to do a story about the toy donation. Could you come over to the bake sale area, please?'

He turned and walked away without her.

Kate ran to catch him up. 'Ivan, what you saw in the staff room was Gary comforting me. I was crying...'

'Not now, Kate.' Ivan's curt reply stalled her. 'Get to work, please.'

Her heart slumped. His cold dismission left her in no doubt. She had hurt him deeply.

With unshed tears welling up behind her eyes, she dragged herself over to the reporter. 'Hi,' she said, pasting on a smile she wasn't feeling. 'How can I help you?'

*

By the end of her shift, a guard entered the staff room and asked for Kate Massey.

'That's me,' she said with a frown when he handed her a small envelope.

'What's this?'

He shrugged. 'Dunno. I was just told to deliver it.'

The short message was from Ivan.

'Kate, sorry, but I'll have to cancel our plans. I can't take you to the pantomime this evening. Regards, Ivan.'

Regards? Kate fumed. She thought he had feelings for her! He couldn't just turn them off like the flick of a switch. She realised he was hurting from what he saw, but he hadn't given her a chance to explain.

'Wait a minute,' she snapped at the messenger. 'I want to send a reply.'

The guy shrugged. 'Whatever.' He flopped on the sofa and scrolled on his phone while Kate routed around for a pen and agonised over what to write.

'Dear Ivan. I'm sorry we can't meet for the pantomime this evening. I was looking forward to spending time with you and meeting your niece. Maybe you can find time in your busy schedule tomorrow to let me explain. What you saw, and what you believed was happening couldn't be further from the truth. I thought we had something special, but maybe I misread you as badly as you did me. Regards, Kate.'

She stuffed the paper into the envelope and passed it to the guy. 'Here. Please make sure he gets this immediately. It's important, okay?' 'Sure,' he said, whistling Frosty the Snowman as he sauntered away.

Kate slumped over the table and

put her head on her arms. Why did the universe keep throwing up more hassle and bad karma with every passing day? Just when she thought she'd turned a corner, everything came crashing down, and she only had one person to blame. Mike Abbott!

Brian wandered inside, still fully dressed in his Santa costume. 'So, Kate. I think I'd be right in saying you must be having one hell of a bad day. Am I right?'

Tears threatened to cascade down her cheeks. 'Yes! I've had better, that's for sure.'

'Then I'm going to drive you home. Do you remember when I said I wear my Santa suit and love to see the kids' faces?'

Kate nodded. 'Yes.'

'It brightens my day, and it will do the same to yours. I think now would be a good time for you to experience that true Christmas feeling of magic and innocence. It'll take your mind off everything that has happened today and rejuvenate your belief in people.'

Kate sighed. The only beliefs she had right now were that Ivan hated her, and Mike was as evil as the devil and out to destroy her. She'd rather go straight home and hide under the duvet, but she knew Brian meant well.

'...and I won't take no for an answer, alright?'

Kate pasted on a smile. 'Brian, that would be lovely.' Her parents had already gone home with all their empty boxes, so a lift home rather than waiting in the snow for a bus was a welcomed idea.

'That's the spirit. Now, do me a favour and keep your pixie suit on. That way, the kids will get an even bigger surprise.'

'Great!' She hoped the heater in his car worked or she would freeze to death!

Brian missed her sarcastic reply. He was already out the door, heading for the car park.

Kate rushed to grab her coat, boots and bag. She needed to catch him up. The car park was enormous. She felt sure she'd never find Brian's car if she didn't hurry.

(How wrong she was!)

Kate jumped into the passenger seat of Brian's white Fiat Panda.

He fiddled with the radio to find some Christmas songs. 'Are you ready to go?'

'Yes,' she said, with a faint smile.

'I'll need directions, Kate. I don't know where you live!'

'Oh, of course!'

The trip was just as Brian had predicted. His car sported a giant snowman fastened to the roof, plus realms of tinsel wrapped around the roof rack, and a small speaker that blurted out Christmas songs.

The children heard the music first, then their eyes popped when they saw the car and who was driving.

Kate felt like royalty as she waved and smiled. The amalgam of expressions she witnessed during the ride filled her with nostalgia for simpler times. She watched the children jumping up and down, clapping and pointing at the snowman, Santa behind the wheel, and his elf in the passenger seat. Their faces, so full of excitement, filled her crying heart with hope. People trudged through the ankle-deep snow, their bodies bent against the biting wind, others laden down with bags, and others walked their dogs, but most still raised a smile as Brian drove past.

Wait, a minute... her eyes narrowed. *Was that...? No! It couldn't be.*

'Brian, wait. That's Mike!' she said.

'Who?' The car screeched to a stop.

'The guy that's bent on ruining my life! Follow him around that corner, please.' She fished in her bag for her phone. 'Do me a favour. Turn off the music. I need to do a bit of surveillance.' She knew it would be difficult with both of them in full costume and a huge snowman strapped on the roof, but it was worth a try. Alison would have been better equipped to do this she realised.

Mike strolled down the street with a chocolate-coloured Labrador by his side, oblivious he was being watched. When the dog squatted to do its business, Kate pressed record and zoomed in. She cursed when Mike extracted a bag to remove the mess.

'This isn't going to plan, Brian.'

'Give it time, Kate. Just wait.'

Mike set off walking again.

Brian inched the car forward.

Kate scrutinised Mike's every move astounded he hadn't noticed the exaggerated car edging slowly behind him.

'He's turned into the street with the angry neighbour!' she informed Brian.

'There, what did I tell you? Patience is a virtue, Kate. Slowly, slowly, catchy monkey.'

She wasn't quite sure what he meant, but intrigued, Kate continued to spy on her nemesis.

Mike crept inside the neighbour's garden, deposited the excrement, and hurried away, throwing the plastic bag over another neighbour's fence.

'Gotcha!' Kate said into the camera before she stopped filming. 'He can't deny that.'

Brian reversed the car.

'What are you doing?'

'I'm taking you home. You have all the evidence you need.'

'But I want to see if he comes back and knocks on the neighbour's door.'

'There's no need. Now, listen, this is what you need to do next....'

*

When Brian dropped her at her gate, she spied her father walking toward her with Sunday.

'Hi, Jellybean. How're you holding up? I should image today wasn't one of your better days?'

'Huh! You could say that again, but as you have always told me, every cloud has a silver lining.'

Alan's eyes narrowed. 'Go on.'

'Brian brought me home in his car.'

Santa waved at him from the driver's seat. 'Yes, I did. You'll never guess what we saw?'

'Tell me.'

'We saw Mike!' Kate replied. 'Not only that, but he was walking a dog.'

'The crafty git. Is it his?'

Kate nodded. 'We think so. But that's not all. He picked up the poop and dumped it in the angry neighbour's garden.'

Alan gasped. 'That's disgusting! Then what?'

'Brian drove away. I mean, we did look rather conspicuous in this.' Her arms opened to show off the snowman car. 'But I managed to take some pictures and a video. I can prove it wasn't me, Dad!'

Alan warmed at the grin radiating from his daughter's face. 'Excellent! So, what are you planning to do?'

'I'm going to get my revenge, dad. And don't even try to talk me out of it!'

Alan ran his finger and thumb across his lips, zipping them together and throwing away the key.

Chapter Nine

Kate gets her Strop on

December 16th

A tap on her door woke Kate up. Alison's head peered around the door. 'Wake up sleepy head, or you are going to be late for work.'

Kate bolted upright. 'What time is it?'

'Calm down. Enough time to get washed and dressed, have a quick breakfast and I'll drive you to the shopping centre.'

Kate exhaled so deeply she thought she was about to blow the covers off her bed.

'So, a little bird told me, you've found out civil servant Mike's got a dog.' Alison grinned.

'Oh, great, you must have heard it through the bug microphone thingamy. Are you up to date now?'

Alison looked sheepish. 'Er. Sorry. No, not exactly. I'm still mega busy.'

'Dad told you?'

'Uh, huh. What's your next move?'

Kate jumped off the bed and ran to her laptop. 'Look at these!' She waggled what looked like a complete A4 pack of papers all printed with photos of Mike. At the top of the page were the words: "This is the neighbour whose dog is fouling the paths of or neighbourhood. Here's the proof!" At the bottom of the page was a link to a YouTube video showing Mike in action and the words, "This proves it has got nothing to do with

Kate Massey."

'Give me one of those. Let me see,' Alison said, beckoning Kate toward her. Alison took a copy, grabbed a pair of scissors, and cut the last sentence off with one clean snip.

'Hey! What did you do that for?'

'He could denounce you for slander. If your name isn't on it, he can't prove you did it.'

Kate nodded. 'You're right. I didn't think about that.'

'You haven't posted the video so everyone will know it's you, have you?'

'No. I created a fake account. But I guess I'll have to be careful when I put the posters up too. If anyone sees me, the same thing could happen.'

'Don't worry about that. I'll put them up, and I'll get dad to help. He's seething with anger about the whole affair.'

Kate hugged her sister. 'Thanks, Alison. You're a star.'

'Uff! No way. Anyway, you're the one that's been on TV. If any of us is close to stardom, it would be you, most definitely. Now, get ready for work, Pixie Peppercorn, or you'll be in trouble with Ivan.'

Kate frowned. 'I'm already in trouble with him.'

Alison laughed.

'What's so funny?'

'Nothing. I just imagined Ivan saying, "Come in, Kate, *Ivan* important issue about your timekeeping to talk to you about."'

Kate groaned. 'Did you listen to the recording when he saw me with Gary in the staffroom?'

'No. I told you; I haven't had time. I must have missed that part. I've been running it on and listening to snippets, but... what were you doing with Gary?'

'Right, well listen to this...'

Kate was almost crying by the time she had finished the story.

Alison opened her arms and enfolded her in a hug.

'Listen to me. Ivan is a great guy, but he's new to this dating business. He's also extremely raw over the death of his wife. He'll hold her in such high esteem that she'll stay on a pedestal for a long time. For him, she was the perfect wife and mother, and she always will be. You have a lot to live up to, Kate. The slightest thing you do to topple his building trust in you will hurt him deeply. It's up to you to be the stronger partner in this relationship.'

'Me?'

'Yes, you! He may be your boss at work, but in your relationship, you must take charge. Control the situation. You have feelings for him, don't you?'

Kate blushed. 'Yeah, I think I'm in love with him, Alison.'

'There you go, then. March into his office and put the record straight. Make him see you are determined to be with him no matter what.'

'Do you think so?'

'Kate, I know so!'

*

Kate pulled back her shoulders exhaled and knocked on the general manager's door.

'Come in.'

Ivan almost gasped when he saw Kate march with determination into his office. She placed both hands on his desk and leaned toward him.

Her eyes were steely cold, her face was flushed, and if he didn't know any better, he would assume she was drunk.

He pushed back his chair, unconsciously leaning further away from her.

'Now, listen to me Ivan Daniels,' she almost snarled. 'I don't know what you think you saw yesterday with me and Gary, but whatever stupid idea you've got in your head, you can erase it right now. Do you hear me? I will say this once and for all. There is nothing, nor will there ever be, anything going on between us... Er... what I'm trying to say is, nothing is going on between Gary and me. I love you! So, get that into your thick head!' She straightened up. 'Now, when you want to apologise, I'll be in the grotto. If I don't see you today, I'll assume it's over.'

As she stomped from the room, Ivan called her back.

'Kate, wait.'

When she turned, she gasped. He stood on the other side of the desk. He stepped closer to her, took hold of her elbows, and his eyes burrowed into hers.

Kate noticed their glassiness as tears welled up.

His head dropped. 'Kate, I'm sorry. I was out of order yesterday. When I found you in Gary's arms, my entire world fell apart. I thought you and I had something special. It hurt me more than I cared to admit that perhaps you didn't feel the same way about me. Sorry,' he said. 'I misjudged you.'

Kate stared into his eyes. Her tears threatened to fall. 'You hurt me, Ivan. I also thought we had a special bond. For you to assume I'd be messing around with Gary offended me deeply. I don't want anyone else.'

Ivan pulled her to him. He kissed her forehead and held her tight. Enfolded in his embrace, Kate's tears of relief coursed down her cheeks. She bit her lip to stop the welling sobs that threatened to overwhelm her.

She blamed her lack of sleep on worrying about him all night.

A member of staff ambled down the corridor with some paperwork, saw the exchange, and dropped the papers on the absent receptionist's desk before making a swift exit.

'Do you still want to go to the pantomime?' Ivan asked, not daring to let her out of his embrace.

'Yes. I'd love to.'

'Great! Then I'll pick you up from your house after work.'

'Okay.' She stared into his eyes, watching them brighten and become alive again.

He leaned in and gently kissed her. When she responded, the kiss deepened until their bodies moulded together, clenched in each other's arms.

A contrived cough pulled them apart.

'Er... Sorry to interrupt, but I need you to sign these papers, Mr Daniels,' the flustered receptionist muttered.

Kate giggled. 'See you later, Ivan,' she said, skipping away.

*

In the changing room, Gary tugged on his elf costume. He felt no more like manning the grotto than having sex with spotty Mary. After consoling Kate the day before, he had assumed he was in with a chance, but the way she had jumped off the sofa when hearing Ivan's voice, he knew she had accepted his affection as condolence and nothing more.

'I'm dreaming of a shite Christmas,' he sang morosely, 'with every manager I fight...'

Carol clicked her tongue. 'Gary, please!'

'He's feeling down in the dumps because Kate snubbed him,' Gemma grinned. 'Boy! Has he got it bad!'

'That's not what happened!' Gary snapped. 'She was upset because *"Ivan* enormous ego" brushed her off. I was just a shoulder to cry on.'

'Yeah,' Gemma replied. 'Accent on the word "just"'.

Annoyed by Gemma's scathing remark, Gary replied, 'Yeah, but at least I know I've always got you to fall back on.'

'What's that supposed to mean?' Gemma's eyes narrowed to slits. She thrust out her chest, lifted her chin and stared at him.

Gary's thin lips converted into a smile. 'Ah, come on Gemma, you know I'll always love ya!'

She sniffed. 'You've got a funny way of showing it!'

He grabbed her by the waist and pulled her to him. 'Come here, Pixie Pumpernickel.' He tickled her around the waist. She was still laughing and screaming when Kate walked inside.

If they hoped to get some adverse reaction, disappointment was heading their way. Kate didn't even notice. Her head was in the clouds. Alison had been so right about everything. The bet was working out well. By answering assertively, she had plunged herself into several situations she would normally have avoided like the plague. Alright, not all the interactions had been positive. She supposed that was to be expected. But Alison's advice that morning had been right on point. Now she knew Ivan loved her. He loved her! Her heart swelled with excitement. She stepped into her pixie costume and went through the motions while her head raced with possibilities.

That night, the Massey household was so enthused with excitement that the dog was running around in circles even quicker than usual.

Alison had helped Kate choose the perfect dress, styled her hair and touched up her make-up. They sat like nervous patients in a dentist's waiting room, anticipating the ring of the doorbell.

Dorothy heard a car and jumped up to peer through the curtains. 'What vehicle does he drive?'

'I don't know. I can't remember!' A flustered Kate replied.

'Some private detective you'd make!' Alison scoffed. She whispered in Kate's ear. 'You better not lose this bet, 'cause I'm not sure I could use you on my team.'

Kate sniffed. 'Thanks a lot!'

Dorothy sat back down just as the doorbell chimed.

A collective gasp reverberated around the living room.

Kate flinched. She ran her hands down her dress. 'Do I look okay?'

Dorothy put the palms of her hands together as if she were praying. 'You look gorgeous! I hope you have the most delightful time.'

'Here, here!' Alan said, grinning at his daughter. 'Knock him dead, Jellybean! ... Not literally, you understand.'

The women laughed.

'You look stunning!' Dorothy reiterated. 'I hope you have a fantastic evening.'

'Thanks, Mum, but I'm only going to watch Aladdin at the church hall, not a West End show.'

'I meant with Ivan. I hope you have a lovely time with him.'

Kate smiled and kissed her. 'Thanks, mum.'

When Kate opened the door, Ivans' lips broke into the biggest smile.

'Kate, you look amazing! Now I feel bad we're just going to a local panto, and I'm not taking you to some top-class venue.'

'Thanks, but the pantomime is fine. Shall we go?'

'Yes, of course.' He cupped her elbow with his hand and walked her to the car.

In the sitting room, three pairs of eyes watched their trajectory from behind the curtains. Kate could sense their vigilance. She didn't look back.

When they arrived at the church hall, Kate wondered if she may have gone over the top in the clothes department. 'I feel rather overdressed,' she said.

Ivan smiled. 'You are the prize rose between a mountain of thorns.' She knew he meant it as a compliment, but it still made her uncomfortable. Almost everyone wore jeans, some with T-shirts, others with a more formal shirt. A handful of women wore dresses, but nothing as elegant as Kate's. She couldn't wait to take her seat. But Ivan had other ideas. Several people came over to say a curious hello. He welcomed them all with a friendly handshake, then turned to present Kate, his eyes sparkling with pride.

By the time they took their seats, Kate felt overwhelmed. Ivan's depth of feeling for her was there for all to see. She only hoped she wouldn't let him down.

He clasped her hand in his as the curtain rose and eagerly pointed out his six-year-old niece who wore the cutest Arabian costume and sat, lower stage right, swaying and clapping with a group of her friends. 'She goes to ballet classes,' Ivan explained. 'She started when she was three, so dancing on a stage is almost second nature to her by now. Aladdin is her first pantomime, though.'

'She's so cute!' Kate replied. 'Can you imagine how great she'd look in the Christmas grotto? Hey, that's an idea. Maybe it's too late for this year, but we could have photo sessions with the kids dressed up next year. That would surely be a big hit. We could have a small wardrobe of costumes. If we did it early enough, parents could use the photos as their Christmas cards.'

Ivan grinned. 'So, you're planning on sticking around for another year, are you?'

Kate's sheepish expression caused him to laugh.

'Well... yeah, I was kind of hoping to stay. But I guess that all depends on you.'

'Good, because I may have a proposition for you.'

'What is it?'

'Just something I've got planned, but I can't tell you yet.'

'Huh! That sounds intriguing.'

'If it comes off, I hope you'll still think it is.'

The music changed, and their eyes returned to the stage where little Amy Bagshot danced as though her life depended on it.

In the interval, Kate met Ivan's parents, sister, and brother-in-law. Ivan presented her as if she was a princess. His family eyed her with amusement and what appeared to be relief.

'Thank goodness!' she heard his father mutter.

His mother shook Kate's hand. With tear-filled eyes and out of Ivan's earshot, she hugged her. 'Thank you so much for putting a smile on my son's face and making him happy again.'

Kate couldn't find the right words to reply. She nodded and smiled. Was she taking on too much? What if she couldn't live up to his and his family's expectations? She fought back the rising panic that threatened to overwhelm her.

After the show, she met Ivan's niece, Amy, who bubbled with excitement with all the praise she received.

'Right! Time to eat,' Ivan's father announced. 'Kate, you must join us. Do you like spicy food? We've booked a table at the Indian restaurant down the street. We love it there!'

The last time she had eaten Indian food had been with her ex. She realised her stomach didn't sink when she thought of him. He was no longer important. Ivan had taken his place in her heart. She had moved on and it felt great. Remembering the hidden microphone, she said, 'YES, I love spicy food.'

'Excellent! You're going to fit in great with us, young lady!' He glanced at his son-in-law. 'Lead the way, Morgan.'

Ivan grabbed Kate's hand and squeezed. He never wanted to let her go.

Two days later, on December 18th, a security guard met Kate at the entrance to the shopping centre. He informed her she should go immediately to Ivan's office.

Unlike the last time that had happened, she was no longer nervous about knocking on his door. When she went inside, his warm grin elated her soul.

'Ah! Just the person I wanted to see.' His eyes sparkled with excitement.

'Why? What is it?'

'I've spoken to Head Office. They already knew about your ideas for the toy collection and everything else you've come up with. I told them you were looking for a more permanent position and they have offered you a job.'

'What? Are you joking? If you are, it isn't funny, Ivan.'

'No, Kate. This is no joke. It's totally legit. I have a contract here. I'd like you to look it over and if you accept, you can start in your new position in the marketing department in January.' He thrust the paperwork into her hands.

Kate couldn't speak. She stared at the contract, hoping this wasn't a dream. 'Are you serious?'

He nodded. 'I've never been more serious about anything in my whole life.' Across his desk, he grabbed her wrists and waited for her eyes to meet his. 'I don't want to lose you, Kate.'

'I... don't know what to say! Thank you so much!' Her mind was racing. Ivan had done this so they could stay together. If she accepted this job, her whole life would change. She could rent her own place, and if she won the bet with Alison, her sister would pay for her to study for a degree. Kate couldn't stop grinning. She could study online.

'What do you think?'

'I accept!' she said.

Ivan's face grew serious. 'Don't make a rash decision, Kate. Take today to think about this carefully. Marketing for a huge shopping centre like this one is no easy feat. You'll be under constant pressure and will need to come up with new ideas to bring in the clientele. I know you can do it, but I want you to consider it carefully.'

'Okay, okay!' She broke free from his grasp and ran around his desk to hug him. 'Ivan, how can I ever thank you? You don't know how this will change my life.'

He held her away from his chest. 'And you don't know how much you've already changed mine.' Bending his head, he kissed her with such passion, Kate thought her feet had left the floor and she was floating. His tongue explored her mouth, and her inner core ignited, filling her body with desire.

When he pulled away, she wanted to beg him not to stop. A small frown furrowed her brow. 'What's wrong?' 'Nothing. I want you to realise what you could gain if you decide to stay.' He gave her a wan smile.

'Ivan! You can't lead me on and then stop! You're killing me!' He grinned, turned her around by the shoulders, and marched her to the door. 'Go to work, Pixie Peppercorn. I'll expect your answer tomorrow in my office.'

Kate glanced at the contract, still not believing her luck. 'I'll be here,' she grinned, skipping down the corridor.

That night, when Kate opened the front door, Alison was waiting for her.

'What is it?'

Her sister sat on the stairs with the wad of printouts in her hands.

'You can't get out this off any longer, Kate. Dad and I have done most of them, but I need help with the rest. I'll give you five minutes and then we're putting the remainder of these up around the neighbourhood.'

When Kate grinned at her rather than sighed with exasperation, Alison's eyes narrowed. 'What're you so happy about?'

'Haven't you heard the recording of my meeting this morning with Ivan?'

Alison shook her head. 'I've told you. I'm up to my ears with work. I'm up to December 10th. But that doesn't let you off the deal. I will listen to them, so don't even think about breaking it.'

Kate's grin grew even bigger. 'That's why I'm smiling. I may not need your deal after all.'

Alison's eyes narrowed even further. 'What are you talking about?' 'Ivan has got me a job!'

'You're joking! No way! Are you serious?'

'Yes, I am. And don't look so surprised. I'm not a complete waste of space you know!'

Dorothy wandered toward them, drying her hand on a tea towel. 'What's all the noise about?'

'You better ask Kate,' Alison said with a disgruntled sniff. She felt so proud of her sister but wanted to play it cool.

'Ask you what, Kate? What's going on?'

'I've got a job, mum.'

'Yes, I know that, dear. You work in the grotto.' She looked across at Alison. 'Is she drunk?'

Alison laughed and shook her head. 'No, mother, she isn't. Unless she's drunk with happiness!'

Kate rolled her eyes in exasperation. 'Mum, I've got a full-time job starting in January.'

'Oh! honey, that's great! Has this got anything to do with Mike? Has he finally repented and got over his silly resentment?'

'Kate refrained from emitting an exasperated sigh. 'No, mum this has got absolutely nothing to do with him,' Alison said.

'It's all down to Ivan,' Kate explained. 'He put my name forward because of all the publicity I've brought to the shopping centre. You are looking at Silver Spring's newest member of the marketing team!'

'Oh! Kate, that's wonderful! What a lovely surprise. You must thank him!'

'I did mum!' Kate glanced across at Alison who was holding in her laughter.

Dorothy spied the fliers. 'So, what're you two up to?'

Alison leaned further forward to cover the posters. 'Nothing. I'm convincing Kate to go for a walk with me.'

Dorothy clicked her tongue. 'Well, you can't take Sunday. Your father went out with him again.' She glanced at her watch. 'That was an hour and a half ago. Goodness knows what he does all that time. I'm beginning to think he's got another woman.'

Kate laughed. 'Our Dad? Are you serious?'

Alison shook her head. 'Don't be ridiculous, mum! Dad would never cheat on you! He's a devoted husband!'

Dorothy sniffed. 'He's up to something. I've got a good mind to… Now, there's an idea. Alison! You could follow him!'

'Me? No, Mum! That's an awful thing to ask of me.' She looked at Kate for support, but she didn't get it. The tables had turned. 'Tell her, Kate!' Alison said.

'I think it might be a good idea,' Kate's grin stretched across her face.

'I'll pay you!' Dorothy blurted out.

'NO! Mother! I'm not spying on my dad. That's…' she shuddered. 'Just wrong!'

Dorothy turned to Kate for support. 'Do you think Alison should do surveillance on her father? Just for an hour? That's all I'm asking.'

Kate's laughing eyes turned to her sister then back to her mum. 'YES,' she replied.

Alison groaned. Her shoulders slumped.

Kate fought back the urge to laugh. It was about time karma placed her sister in an awkward situation for once.

Dorothy's tea towel flicked toward Alison. 'Go on. Go now! You might be able to find him if you act quickly.'

'Mother, let's get one thing straight. I'm the detective, not you. These things take time. Kate and I will go for a walk and if, by some twist of fate we see him, then I'll see what I can do.'

'Hey! Don't drag me into this,' Kate said. 'I don't want to be creeping around spying on my dad!'

Alison's eyes turned to steel, but her lips twisted into a scary grin. 'Kate, I'm only going to ask you this once. Will you help me?'

Her sister had no choice but to agree. 'Yes,' she sighed.

Oblivious to the mounting tension, Dorothy clapped her hands together. 'Lovely!'

Kate changed her shoes for sturdy boots and joined her sister on their walk. 'Nice move,' she said.

Alison smirked. 'Yeah, well, I knew you had to agree.'

'Maybe I don't anymore. I've got myself a full-time job.'

'Hey! You can't break the deal like that! You agreed to do it until the stroke of midnight. I'm holding you to that!'

'But.'

'No buts! I'll still uphold my end of the bargain. You've got to do the same. I think Ivan's great, but as mum says, don't put all your eggs in one basket. Don't become dependent on him. Have your own life, your own money and your own ideas. You can't assume you'll be with him forever. That was the mistake you made with your ex. You need to be independent. If you complete the bet, I'll get you a flat and I'll still pay for your university studies, but only if you complete this.'

Kate groaned. 'Okay, okay! It's exceedingly generous of you, Alison.' Her eyes narrowed. 'What do you get out of this?'

Alison feigned offensiveness. 'Me? I get to see my little sis happy for once. I can set her up and let her make a success of her life. Although I must admit you're doing a pretty good job of that on your own at present.'

Kate smiled. 'Thanks, but that's down to you. If I were truthful, there are several occasions when I definitely wouldn't have answered in the affirmative. It's because of your bet that things have turned out so well. And I...'

'Shush!' Alison's arm flew out and hit Kate across the waist. She dragged her sister behind a huge oak tree. 'Look!'

Kate's mouth dropped open. Their dad was leaving a house a little further down the street. Sunday jumped up and down on the spot, like one of Santa's reindeer impatient to fly.

'Who lives there?' Kate whispered.

Alison shrugged in reply. They both gasped when a young woman appeared in the doorway. She wore a long, multicoloured cheesecloth dress that displayed her bare shoulders. The faint tinkling of tiny bells on the hem of the garment reached the girls' ears on the other side of the street. Her hair had that tousled, just got out of bed, look. She had gathered it together and stuck what appeared to be a long wooden dowel through the middle of it.

Oblivious he was being watched, Alan turned and waved goodbye. Then he walked down the path with a huge smile on his face and Sunday jumping by his side.

'I can't believe it!' Kate said, as Alison opened the nearest garden gate and dragged her inside. They hid behind the bushes.

'I would never have thought it possible. My dad, of all people, is having an affair!' Kate said, shaking her head.

'Just hold your horses there a minute, little sis. You can't jump to conclusions. There could be a perfectly rational reason he was there.' She paused. 'I can't think of one off the top of my head, but, in my business, you can't jump to conclusions. You have to work on facts. It looks like I'll have even more work cut out.'

'Some Christmas this is going to be if dad is having an affair! Kate gasped and grabbed Alison's arm. 'You don't think he'll leave her, do you? A lot of couples split up over the holiday period.'

'Lots of people commit suicide over Christmas too, but you can't assume that's going to happen here either. We need facts, undeniable proof. We can't assume anything or accuse him of something that may not be true.'

'You're right, but it puts a downer on Christmas already. I can't sit around the table wondering if dad is about to drop a bombshell.'

'Come on,' Alison nudged her sister. 'Let's get out of this garden before someone spots us and has us arrested.'

They scampered back into the street, scurried to the end of it and continued sticking the condemning posters of Mike the disgruntled civil servant all over the neighbourhood.

When they reached the house where the angry man had confronted Kate, she stopped. 'This home belongs to the guy who accused me of the crime.'

Alison lifted her chin and scanned the façade of the building. 'Yeah? Right then. It's time we had a chat with him, don't you think, Kate?'

Kate stared at her sister, astounded at how she had cunningly twisted her statement into a question. She sighed, cringing inside. 'Yes. If you say so.'

Alison leaned in and cupped one hand behind her ear. 'Sorry? What did you say? Was that a yes?'

Through gritted teeth, Kate replied, 'Yes.'

'That's a good girl. Now, come on. Let's get this sorted out once and for all. After what we've just seen, I'm wound up enough to deal with this arrogant old guy.'

Kate clutched her diminishing pile of posters and forced herself to swallow. She hoped Alison would play the leading role in the interaction. Confrontations had never been her thing. That's why her ex-boyfriend had walked all over her.

Alison knocked on the door. She wasn't about to face him with full guns blazing. She would play it by ear. If they could talk rationally about the situation, that would be better for everyone involved.

'Did you hear that?' Kate said. 'I thought I heard a moan.'

'Are you sure?'

'Yeah. Listen.'

Alison knocked again. 'Is there anyone there?'

An agonising groan reached their ears.

'Oh, my God! I think he's hurt,' Alison said. 'I'll phone for an ambulance and the police. Then I'll ask the neighbours if they have a spare key.'

'I'll walk around the house. See if I can get inside.'

'Be careful, Kate, you don't want to get done for breaking and entering.'

Kate nodded. She felt terrible. Despite her caustic interaction with the man, she wouldn't want anything horrible to happen to him.

At the back door, she tried the handle and was surprised to find it unlocked. She opened the door and stuck her head inside.

'Hello? Are you okay?'

'Help me!'

Hearing the faint cry coming from the kitchen, she strode inside. On the floor, she found him. He explained he had been carrying a pan of water to the stove. Some must have spilt out onto the floor, and he had slipped on it.

'I couldn't get up. I've been here for hours.'

Kate didn't like the look of his leg. It jutted out in a weird position. The cold water had seeped into his clothes, and he was shivering.

She dropped to her knees, falling into the puddle of water, but not caring. 'Hold on. You'll be alright. My sister has called an ambulance.'

The man groaned and closed his eyes. 'Thank you so much,' he said.

'Don't take this wrong, but I'm going to have to remove your clothes. I need to get you warm. Is that okay?'

The man kept his eyes closed but nodded.

The emergency services arrived to find Kate had stripped off his cardigan, shirt and vest but left his trousers. She didn't want to move his twisted leg. She had turned on the oven and was rubbing him dry with a big thick towel. She realised how weird it must look. A young woman undressing the injured person, but the paramedics praised her for her actions.

When Alison confirmed she was a private detective, the police entrusted the house keys to her.

Kate held the old man's hand and said she'd go with him to the hospital.

'Don't worry. My sister will make sure your house is secure and I'll stay with you, alright?'

He bowed his head. 'Thank you. Thanks so much. Both of you.'

'Anytime,' Kate replied. 'You just hang on in there, okay?'

'Yes,' he muttered.

For Kate, the situation put things into perspective. If they hadn't called round, the old man's condition could have had dire consequences. The predicament trivialised the whole doggie-doo incidents.

Alison eventually arrived at the hospital. She had put a small bag of his possessions together, including his phone, some money, a book she had found on his bedside table, some toiletries, his slippers and clean pyjamas.

'I'll hang on to your house keys if that's alright, then I can water your plants and check the house is safe while you're in hospital. I've also brought you some grapes, and my mum has given me a box of mince pies for you. I hope you like them, Mr…'

'Alison, his name is Arthur,' Kate explained. 'He lost his wife to cancer last year. This will be his first Christmas without her.' She didn't mention how, when he had calmed down, he had recognised who she was. Arthur had apologised profusely for how he had spoken to her. He blamed his wife's demise and admitted he was angry with the world.

Kate didn't go into detail. She didn't think it was the right time. She accepted his apology for shouting at her but didn't mention Mike and his swindle.

As the trio sat talking, a passerby strode past and then stopped. 'Kate? Kate Massey isn't it?'

Kate looked up and nodded. She didn't recognise the young man. 'I'm Dave Green, the freelance reporter and photographer who took the shots of you for the toy collection in the Shopping Centre.'

'Oh yes, I remember you,' Kate said.

'What're you doing here?'

'Oh, we found Arthur on the kitchen floor. He'd fallen over in the kitchen and broken his leg.'

'These girls saved my life!' Arthur rasped, his eyes overflowing with tears. 'I can never thank them enough.'

Smelling a good story, Dave extracted his note pad. 'Arthur, how would you like to be in the local paper?' he began.

*

December 19th

'I don't believe it! This is so great!' Dorothy enthused over the Christmas pop song blaring out from the tiny radio in the kitchen. 'Both my daughters are listed as heroes in the local paper. Incredible! And what a fabulous photo!' She held up the newspaper like she was giving a classroom demonstration. 'I'm going to frame this. How many copies did you get, Alan?'

'Ten,' he said, grinning behind his bacon sandwich. He picked a piece from his plate and discreetly passed it to Sunday who barked, licked his lips and swallowed the sliver of meat as if he hadn't eaten since last Christmas.

Dorothy was too excited to inform him not to feed the dog at the table. 'Wait until Ivan sees this! He'll be more infatuated with you than ever, Kate.'

Her daughter squirmed with embarrassment. 'Mum!'

'Don't worry about that, Mother,' Alison replied. 'Ivan is already smitten. I can tell.'

Kate guessed her sister had caught up a bit with the recordings. She squirmed with embarrassment, thinking Alison could also hear their most intimate moments. She read the article and felt pleased Dave Green had heeded her request and mentioned the Shopping centre and toy collection again. Ivan would be pleased.

'Kate, don't worry about taking the bus, this morning. I'll drive you to Silver Springs myself,' Dorothy said. 'I've er... got some shopping to do and other things.'

'Great! Thanks, Mum,' Kate said, tucking into her bacon sandwich. 'It'll be lovely not having to traipse to the bus stop in this cold weather.' Little did she know her mother had an ulterior motive for her generosity.

*

Mike had only taken a few steps out of his garden when he saw the first flier. His blood boiled with embarrassment. There could be no doubt the photos were of him. And the likelihood of anyone else taking them other than that stupid Kate was also not an option.

'I hate you, Kate Massey.' The name barely escaped from behind his clenched jaw. Embarrassment didn't seem a strong enough noun to explain how humiliated and astounded he felt. He looked down at his dog. He couldn't take the fliers down with the Labrador at his side. That was even more evidence he was the guilty party.

At a run, he returned the dog to the house and raced back to the street. He ripped the first offending flier from the lamp-post and crumpled it into his fist. How he wished it was Kate's head! When he glanced down the street. He felt sick. There were yellow fliers everywhere. It would take him ages to remove them all. He set off at a jog, ripping them from walls, noticeboards and posts as if his life depended on it.

*

'Here, you go, dear,' Dorothy said as she parked as close to the shopping centre entrance as she could. 'You haven't far to walk now in all that snow and sludge. I just hate that.'

'Hate what?'

'The sludge, dear. When the snow's melting, it's like one of those drinks you get in the summer that's full of crushed ice. I hate it because not only is it melted snow, but it's all dirty and grey-coloured.'

'Yeah, you wouldn't want to drink that!'

'No way!'

'I supposed it would be better than yellow snow, though, wouldn't it?'

'What? Urgh!' Dorothy laughed. 'Yes. That's true. I definitely wouldn't want to drink that!'

They strolled arm in arm into the centre.

'Right then,' Dorothy said, suddenly sounding authoritative and looking a little shifty. 'I'll leave you to it.' She clutched the newspaper inside her shopping bag.

'Are you alright, mum?' Kate had noticed her sudden change in demeanour.

'Huh? Oh, yes, dear. Never been better! Bye now.'

Kate's brow furrowed. Familiar with her mother's sneaky ways, she knew Dorothy was up to something. Kate wondered what it was.

When she entered the staff room, she found Gemma and Mary squinting at the local newspaper.

'Well, well, well, if it isn't Pixie Peppercorn and her penchant for the papers.' Gemma's tone was full of sarcasm. A cruel smirk turned her thin lips into a grimace. 'I wouldn't put it past you to have broken the guy's leg on purpose or bribed him into saying you helped him!' Gemma snarled. 'What's a penchant?' Mary asked.

'Yeah, do you even know what that means?' Kate asked. 'I must admit I'm surprised it's part of your vocabulary, or did you have to look it up beforehand?'

Gemma threw the newspaper onto the table. She slumped back on the sofa, folded her arms, and crossed her legs. An exasperated sigh passed her lips. 'Stupid cow!' she muttered.

Kate ignored her.

'Hey! Be careful with that! I haven't read it yet,' Carol said from her permanent position by the counter, stirring mugs of tea.

Gary sauntered inside singing, "All I want for Christmas is flu," then feigned a sneeze into an oversized handkerchief. He didn't get the laugh he had been expecting.

'What's up?'

When Gemma's leg started pumping up and down and he registered her face, he wished he'd never asked.

Carol supplied him with the information. She pointed to the discarded newspaper in the centre of the table. 'Kate's got herself in the newspaper again. This time with her sister. They helped an old man who had fallen and broken a leg.'

Gary lifted his chin in reply, then sauntered over to the table and picked up the creased paper.

Gemma's leg pumping increased in speed the longer he read. The more it moved, the less he could concentrate.

'Carol, is one of those teas for me? I'm as parched as my sad effort of a Christmas tree languishing in my flat.'

She nodded and bustled over.

'Thank you, my good woman. I've been thinking. You should change your surname to Singer, then everyone would call you Carol Singer!' He guffawed at his wit.

Carol giggled. 'I'd have to sing everywhere I go!'

Gemma clicked her tongue in annoyance and her leg

pumped even faster. 'Better you than Kate. She could clear a room in twenty seconds. Her voice could cut paper!'

Gary frowned. 'Gemma, can you please stop jiggling your leg like that? Anyone would think you were drilling for oil!'

Kate chortled, but Gemma's rage reached boiling point.

'I hate you, Gary! You get right on my nerves!'

His demeanour softened. 'Hey, come on, Gemma. I'm only playing with you.' He placed the newspaper on the table, then walked over and dropped beside her. His strategically placed hand on her knee stopped the pumping action – to everyone's relief.

'So, tell me, Pixie Pumpernickel, what plans have you got for Christmas Eve?'

Gemma couldn't look at him. 'Dunno.'

'WHAT!' he said in exaggerated disbelief. 'That can't be right. A beautiful young woman like you can't stay at home on Christmas Eve. I tell you what, why don't you come out with me? I've been invited to a friend's Christmas party in the centre of town, and I'd hate to go alone.' He leaned closer and batted his puppy dog eyes. 'Come on, Gems, say you'll come.' He stuck out his bottom lip for added effect.

A sly smile spread across her face as she squirmed on the sofa. Her eyes met his. 'Alright!'

Gary jumped up. 'Yeah! Sorted. Nice one.'

Carol broke up their interaction. 'Come on, everyone. Time to go to work.'

As they sauntered through to the changing room, Gary pulled Kate aside. 'I'll drop her like a stone if you'll come with me instead.'

Kate smiled and rubbed his arm. 'Sorry. I already have plans.' His shoulders slumped and his bottom lip stuck out. 'Elf

Edelweiss will be very upset.'

'He'll get over it!' Kate laughed.

*

'Come in!' Ivan shouted when he heard the knock on the door.

'Ivan! How lovely to see you again,' Dorothy stood brandishing a copy of the local newspaper as if it were a weapon of war and she intended to bludgeon him to death.

He sprang to his feet. 'Mrs Massey, what a pleasant surprise. Come in. Sit down.'

When Dorothy smiled and complied, Ivan's blood pressure returned to normal.

'Here,' she said, thrusting the paper into his hands. 'I wanted to give you this. Or have you already read it?'

'No. What is it?'

'Look at page eight. Kate's in the newspaper again. This time with her sister!' Her voice rose towards the end of the sentence, betraying her pride. 'They helped an elderly man who had fallen and broken his leg. But being the professional she is, our Kate even got them to mention Silver Springs Shopping Centre in the article.'

He read the article in silence while Dorothy fiddled in her shopping bag.

'Wow! Your daughter never ceases to amaze me. May I keep this?' He squinted closely at the photograph. A frisson of a frown visited his brow. Doubt flew through his mind.

Dorothy, still preening from her daughter's success pushed a plastic container across his desk. 'Here. These are for you. It's a sort of mini hamper. A few mince pies, a piece of chocolate log, some shortbread biscuits iced to look like Christmas trees, and a piece of the Christmas cake you liked so much the other day.'

'How kind of you. Thank you very much!'

Dorothy nodded but didn't give him the chance to continue. 'She never used to be like this, you know.'

'Sorry. What?'

'Kate. She was never self-assured and motivated like she is now. You have inspired her to step out of her comfort zone. She's always been introverted and subdued, letting people, including her ex, walk all over her. But, I don't know, since she got this job, she's changed and I believe that's all thanks to you. So, I'm here to show my appreciation. I'd like you to confirm your invitation to our house for Christmas day. And I won't take no for an answer,' she said when Ivan tried to interrupt.

'Dorothy. That would be lovely, but there's something I need to discuss with you first...'

*

Mike had seen the secretary leave her post. He was about to approach Ivan's office when he heard Dorothy laughing and saying her goodbyes. He quickly shot down the flight of stairs and dived into a gents' clothes shop until she had gone past.

Still seething over Kate's poster campaign, he was determined to humiliate her as she had humiliated him. After careful thought, he knew exactly what he needed to do. He sprinted up the stairs and knocked on Ivan's door.

'Come in!'

Mike marched straight in. He found Ivan munching on a mince pie and reading the article about Kate and her sister.

'Oh, hello, Ivan. Do you remember me? We met at The Duchess restaurant last week.'

'Oh, yes, of course. How can I help you?'

'I'm afraid I'm here with bad news. You may remember I work at the job centre in the high street.'

'Oh, yes, I remember Kate telling me something about that. Isn't it down to you she got this job?'

Mike's lips narrowed at the memory. 'Yes. That's correct.'

'So, what do you want to tell me?'

'It has come to our attention that Kate has got a criminal record for embezzlement and fraud.'

'Sorry, what?' Ivan dropped the confectionary as if it had burnt his fingers.

'I felt it was my duty to inform you as soon as possible. She is a master manipulator who charms anyone in her path to get what she wants. And that's money. Lots of it.' He pointed at the newspaper article. 'The police are looking into this case, too. It's weird how both sisters,' his fingers imitated inverted commas, 'just happened to find him, in his house on his own. The police have reason to believe they were casing the joint.'

Ivan remained silent. He didn't want to believe Mike's sordid accusations, but as the general manager, it was his responsibility to vet the people he employed. He hadn't run a background check when he offered her the job, as she was only supposed to be in the store until Christmas and they needed someone quickly. But if Mike's accusations were true, Kate had wheedled her way under Ivan's skin, and he had fallen for it.   His heart thumped faster. He'd got her a permanent job at the centre! His mind was in turmoil. Had she been playing him from the beginning? He found it hard to comprehend what Mike said was true. He hadn't forgotten the civil servant held a grudge against her about a school dance or something trivial, but Ivan knew that as general manager he would be held accountable, and he had to get this information checked out.

His stomach flipped. He remembered his conversation with Dorothy. He had involved her in a Christmas surprise for Kate. What if the whole family were in on the scam? It didn't bear thinking about! If it were true, he could lose his job for incompetence.

Mike could see his confusion and revelled in it. 'If I were you, Ivan, I'd stay well away from the entire family. They're nothing but trouble. All of them.' He basked in Ivan's discomfort. This had gone better than he had hoped. 'Well, I'll leave you to it. I just thought it was my duty to tell you especially as she pushed me to set up the job interview to begin with.'

Ivan nodded. Lost for words, his eyes fell on the newspaper photograph. He had doubted himself before, but now he was almost certain he had interviewed Kate's sister for the position, not Kate. He had felt nothing strangely resembling sexual attraction during the interview, but the next time he had seen her, her captivating green eyes had enmeshed him. Then it hit him like a head-on collision. He presumed the sisters must have changed places because Alison knew she wasn't getting through to him.

His head fell into his hands. Kate had pulled him out of the deep depression he had lived in since his wife's death. Would she purposefully do something so cruel? He swore if this was a scam, he would hide away in his office and never date another woman as long as he lived.

With a heavy heart, he reached for the phone.

Mike trotted down the stairs, shoved his hands in his pockets and with a grin on his face sang along to the Christmas music blaring from the speakers. His sense of accomplishment overwhelmed him. *Take that, Kate Massey!* he repeated over and over in his head.

*

After work, Alison met Kate at the entrance to the shopping centre. They had both agreed to visit Arthur in the hospital.

Kate had stopped at a couple of stores to buy some sweets, and a few magazines to help him pass the time. As she was leaving, she glanced up at Ivan's office. He stood at the window, watching them.

Kate raised a hand and waved. Her smile fell from her face when he stared at her with an expression she could only describe as loathing. He turned and walked away.

'Did you see that?'

Alison nodded. 'What's his problem?'

'I don't know, but something is wrong.'

'That may be, but you'll have to find out tomorrow. I want to get this hospital visit over and done with. You know I hate the smell of those places.'

Kate nodded. Deep in thought, she followed her sister outside. Something had upset him, but what?

Arthur graced them both with a huge smile and clapped his hands together. 'My two guardian angels! How are you?'

'Never mind how we are. We want to know how you're doing,' Alison said.

'Not bad at all, considering. The doctor said I can go home

tomorrow.'

'That's excellent news!' Kate replied. 'But how will you manage?'

Arthur's smile slid from his face. He looked at the bedcovers and sighed. 'I hadn't thought about that. I'll get by, somehow.'

'Nonsense!' Alison replied. 'You'll come back to our mum and dad's. We can't leave you all alone.'

'No,' Kate agreed. 'Especially not a Christmas time.'

'But…'

'No buts, Arthur. It's settled. I'll pick you up tomorrow and take you to ours. You can have my bedroom. I only stay there occasionally. And if need be, I can crash on the couch.'

'Are you sure?'

'I'm positive! We can't have you hobbling around your house at Christmas time,' Alison said.

'But what about your parents?'

'They'll love it,' Kate replied. 'Mum's great at mollycoddling people and I think that's exactly what you need. And dad is the most laid-back person you could ever meet.'

A stream of fat tears coursed down his cheeks. 'Thank you so much, girls. You are both a credit to your generation.'

'Stop crying right now!' Alison said. 'Otherwise, you'll set Kate off and once she starts, she can't stop!'

'Hey! Neither can you!'

Arthur laughed at their sibling rivalry. 'Okay, okay! I'll come. Thank you, girls,' he said.

The following day, December 20th, Alison dropped Kate at work, then went to the hospital to pick up Arthur. When she arrived, he was sitting in a wheelchair at the entrance to the hotel. A hospital porter was chatting to him.

'Hi,' Alison said. 'I'm here for Arthur.' She saw the tears of gratitude welling up behind his eyes. 'Arthur, don't you dare cry!' she said, although his actions melted her heart. She realised how terrible it must be to be alone, especially at Christmas, and even more so if you were ill or injured. 'Come on. Let's get you in the car.'

He sat in the back; it was easier, and he could stretch out his broken leg. The hospital porter passed him two crutches and wished him a Merry Christmas.

Once Alison drove into the traffic, she looked at him through the rearview mirror. 'I was thinking. Would you like to go to your house first and get some of your things before I take you to my parents' house? You know, clean clothes, pyjamas, etcetera.'

'That would be great, Alison. Thank you.'

'No trouble.'

Getting him out of the car proved just as fiddly as putting him in, but they managed it. She followed behind him up the garden path and then went in front to open the door.

Arthur stepped inside and sighed. Tears once again made an appearance, but Alison chose to ignore them. She knew he was glad to be back, but the ordeal had overwhelmed him.

'Now, Arthur, you tell me what you want, and I'll get it all for you. But first, I'm going to put the kettle on. You'll feel better with a nice cup of tea.'

Arthur smiled; his eyes pierced hers. You're so kind, Alison. Thank you.'

As Alison ran around collecting all his belongings, Arthur sat at the kitchen table with his mug of tea. His eyes fell on the yellow poster folded into four. When he opened it, he couldn't believe what he saw. Anger rose inside him like a pressure cooker reaching its limit. His neighbour, Mike, had duped him. Arthur had said some horrible things to Kate because he'd believed everything Mike had told him. He had never thought to question it. Yet despite all of that, she had rallied around to help him in his hour of need.

When Alison returned to the kitchen, she found him sobbing.

'Arthur, what's wrong?'

He held up the flier. 'Why didn't you tell me?'

Alison shrugged. 'Because with everything that happened, it seemed so unimportant.'

'But I believed him. I wouldn't listen to your sister, and she had told me the truth all along!'

'Yes, but don't worry about it. It's in the past now.'

'Huh! It may be for you, but not for me. He hasn't heard the last of this, let me tell you!'

Alison remained silent. It wasn't in her character to slander a person - unless she was paid to do it - but Mike needed his comeuppance, and she was pretty sure feisty Arthur would make sure he got it.

'I think I've got everything, Arthur,' she said, changing the subject. 'Are you ready to go to my parents' house now?'

He took his last swig of tea. 'Yes, my dear. I believe I am, and I'll never be able to thank you enough.'

*

Ivan hung around his office all day, like some sort of hermit waiting for the head office to get back to him. It was killing him not knowing if he had fallen in love with a con artist. He also felt bad that he could even consider Kate to be that type of person. Preoccupied, he drummed a pencil on top of his desk, urging the phone to ring, but the only ringing tone he heard was the Christmas bells in the shopping centre.

All day long, he had avoided Kate, but it was killing him. He wanted to see her. Hell, he needed to spend time with her. She was like an illicit drug he had become hooked on and couldn't get enough.

He crossed his office and stared into the grotto below. She looked so cute in her pixie costume as she danced to the Christmas pop songs and interacted with the children and parents. He would describe her as pretty, yet vulnerable.

After watching her for almost ten minutes, he decided it was more than doubtful she could keep up the pretence twenty-four-seven. But she only had to fool him, not the hundreds of shoppers swarming the shopping centre.

His mind went back to Mike. A guy she had jilted at a school dance a hundred years ago. How could the guy still hold a grudge after all that time? Then he remembered Kate telling him about the problem with her dog, Mike and the angry neighbour. It stood to reason the guy must have a mental disorder. He couldn't be right in the head! The shrill ring of the telephone made him jump. 'Hello...?' 'Ah, Ivan, sorry to ring so late in the day. We've had technical problems with the computers all day long. It's been a complete nightmare! Anyway, I've run the search, and I can't find anything dodgy about Kate, her sister or anyone in her family. Not even an unpaid parking ticket. They're all as clean as a whistle. Don't you think that's a weird expression? How would anyone or anything be compared to a whistle? I mean they're hardly a clean item at the best of times, are they? They're full of spit!' Ivan had stopped listening. His heart soared with relief and happiness. Kate wasn't playing with him. Her affection was genuine. 'Yeah, thanks, Len. That's great. Bye now.' He grabbed his jacket and ran down the stairs. Once he reached the grotto, he jumped the fence, pulled Kate into his arms and kissed her.

Ecstatic but embarrassed, Kate wanted to pull away. Her knees went weak with the fervour of his kiss. Her head felt dizzy. She clung to him.

A rising 'Woo Hoo!' echoed around the centre followed by rapturous applause.

When he finally pulled away, Kate stared at him in surprise. 'Ivan,' she said, blushing with embarrassment. 'What are you doing?'

'I'm showing everyone who cares to look how much I love you.' His eyes searched hers for understanding.

'I love you too,' she almost whispered. 'But next time, let's do this in less public surroundings, alright?'

'Sure! Now, get out of that costume. I'm taking you out for dinner.' He turned to Carol who stood grinning and clapping. 'Carol, can you manage without Kate for the last forty minutes?'

'Yes, of course, Mr Daniels.'

Gemma seethed with annoyance while Mary said, 'Ahh!' with her hands on her heart.

Gary hung his head in defeat. He couldn't compete with a general manager. He turned to Gemma and smiled. 'How about you and me grabbing a burger after work?'

Gemma eyed him with suspicion. 'Why?'

'Because I like you, that's why.' He nudged her in the ribs. 'But you knew that already, didn't you?'

Her eyes searched his. She didn't want to be used, then tossed aside — again! Was he doing this to make Kate jealous?

'Come on,' he batted his doleful puppy dog eyes. 'What do you say?'

I am hungry, she thought, *and if you're paying, why not?*

'Okay...' she replied, batting her eyelashes and giving him a seductive smile.

At the restaurant, Ivan and Kate ate a hearty meal of scallops for starters, roast beef in a brandy sauce, roasted potatoes with a julienne of vegetables for the main course, with Christmas pudding and custard for dessert. When they had finished, Ivan grew quiet. He fiddled with his linen serviette and avoided eye contact.

Kate experienced a sense of unrest. She guessed something unpleasant was coming. She reached across the table and placed her hand on his forearm.

'Ivan, what is it?'

His eyes met hers. She perceived his discomfort.

He took a deep breath.

From the length of his inhalation, Kate further convinced herself she wouldn't like what he said.

'Kate, I never want there to be any secrets between us, so I have to tell you something. It's not nice, but I must reveal what has happened today.'

Kate's stomach squeezed so tightly, she thought she might throw up. 'What is it, Ivan?'

He paused, hardly making eye contact with her.

Fear crept up her spine. Scared, she couldn't imagine what he was about to say.

'Mike Abbott came to my office this morning.'

'Ugh! Him! What did he want?'

'Here's the thing. He came to slander you.'

'He did WHAT?' Her voice rose several octaves. Other diners stared in their direction.

Ivan patted her arm. 'Please, Kate, just hear me out.'

'What did he say?' Her words barely passed through her thinning lips, and her fingernails clawed the tablecloth bunching it into her palms.

Ivan bit his lip. He regretted starting the conversation in a public place. He should have waited until they were in his car.

Kate's eyes bore into him, like a lioness about to move in for the kill.

He cupped her hand over his. 'He said it had come to his attention that you have a criminal record for embezzlement and fraud.' Ivan squeezed her hand when he saw the anger rising in her eyes. He didn't want to tell her Mike had slandered her entire family unit, but he had said he'd be honest.

Kate sat seething and speechless. 'I can't believe this!' she whispered, shaking her head. Tears formed behind her eyes.

'There's more.'

Kate's eyes leaked. 'What?' tears travelled down her cheeks. She pulled her hand from Ivan's and swiped them away.

'He accused your entire family of being con artists. He said you were hanging around me because you smelled money, but your emotions were false. You were with me for what you could gain from the relationship.'

'But that's not true, Ivan. I'm in love with you!' Overwhelmed by the situation and her confession of her true feelings, she needed to escape. She reached for her handbag. 'I'd better go.'

Ivan grabbed the straps of her bag. 'No, Kate. You are not going anywhere. You're the best thing that's happened to me for a long time, and I'm not about to let you walk out of my life. Now, please. Sit down.'

His words pulled at her heartstrings. She slumped back into her seat, searching his eyes for sincerity.

'Listen to me. Kate. I'm obliged to follow up on any information I'm given that could damage the shopping centre's reputation. I called the head office. They have confirmed that everything Mike said was a lie.'

Kate gritted her teeth. She understood he had criteria and rules to follow, but it still hurt that her whole life and those of her family members had been pecked over and scrutinised by others. Her hatred for Mike grew to humongous proportions.

Ivan guessed what was running through her mind. When her eyes darkened, he knew her thoughts were on Mike Abbott.

'Don't think I'll let Mike get away with this unscathed,' Ivan said. 'He's pushed the boundaries too far and I'll make sure he reaps the consequences.' He paused. 'Now, seeing as we are telling the truth here, I would like to ask you a question and I need you to answer honestly, okay?'

'Yes,' Kate said, close to sobbing her heart out and to hell with whoever was watching.

'It's about your sister.'

Kate blanched. Had he found something out about her that was illegal after all? No, it couldn't be. He had said they were all clean. Her stomach tightened even further.

'I won't be angry. I just want the truth.'

He watched her nod her head and registered the fear in her eyes. 'Was it Alison I interviewed for the job?'

'Yes!' her stomach relaxed, and her shoulders slumped. She had imagined something much worse. She didn't know what, but the question was easy for her to answer. 'I'm sorry! I chickened out. I'm useless at interviews and as we look vaguely similar, Alison said she'd pretend to be me. But we didn't intend to trick you. I was just desperate for work. My mum had threatened to find me a job herself if I didn't get one in ten days. You don't know her like we do. I mean, I love her of course, but she's a domineering woman who always gets her way!'

Ivan thought back to Dorothy's visit to his office and smiled. 'Yeah, I know.'

Kate frowned. 'How did you find out that it was Alison and not me?'

'Your mum showed me your photo in this morning's newspaper.'

'She came to your office? I knew she was up to something!'

He nodded. 'When I saw the photo of you both together, it all made sense. The only difference is I didn't feel attracted to your sister, but the first time I saw you, I couldn't think of anyone else.'

Kate smiled through fresh tears. 'So, you're not angry?'

'How can I be angry when I've found the woman I want to spend the rest of my life with?'

Kate jumped up. She flung herself into his lap and threw her arms around his neck. 'Thank you, Ivan. That's the nicest thing anyone has ever said to me.'

Embarrassed by the nosey diners, Ivan extracted her arms from around his neck. 'Alright, Kate. Let's get you home. It's another long day at the grotto for you tomorrow.'

'As if I'll be able to sleep now. Ivan, you're killing me!'

'Yeah, killing you with kindness,' he said.

*

December 21st saw all the shopping centre workers on a high. After work that evening was the annual Christmas party, hosted by the owners of the centre. They invited all shop holders and centre staff workers to the affair.

'It's a big event, Kate,' Carol explained as Pixie Peppercorn curled her lip.

'I'm not a big partygoer.'

'Ivan will be there. You really should go.'

Kate gave a reluctant nod. His being there was a definite incentive, and when she remembered that in January, she would be there every day, Kate thought perhaps she ought to make an effort. She should show her face and introduce herself to the rest of her new workmates.

It felt weird finishing her shift then going home only to return all dressed up in elegant evening wear, and no pixie suit in sight.

Her family and Arthur had all expressed their opinion as to how beautiful she looked in her black evening dress, matching high-heels and shoulder wrap.

Alison had taken the night off work to drive her there. Kate had tried to coax her into joining the party too, but Alison wouldn't hear of it. 'I've still got most of your recordings to catch up on. Tonight might be my chance.' The management had booked one of the restaurants within the shopping centre for the event. The room was beautifully decorated with garlands, holly and a huge Christmas tree resplendent with beautiful ornaments, tinsel and multicoloured flashing lights. A small band had set up in the corner and were playing upbeat Christmas pop songs to welcome everyone as they entered.

Kate felt a little uncomfortable on her arrival. She didn't recognise anyone.

'Hey! Peppercorn! Over here!' Gary stood with the girls.

Putting her arm through his, Gemma locked eyes with Kate. An instinctive measure to prove he was hers.

Kate said hello and complemented Gemma on her outfit, attempting to show she held no malice towards her.

Gemma didn't look so convinced, but she gave Kate a half-hearted smile. 'Thanks,' she said.

'I'll get you a drink, Kate. What do you fancy?' Gary said, much to Gemma's chagrin.

'Ooh, thank you. A white wine please,' Kate replied, relieved she wouldn't have to push her way to the bar. 'How much do you think it'll be?' she opened her clutch bag, looking for her purse.

Carol laughed. 'Kate! It's a party! The management has paid for everything!'

'Oh!' Kate blushed, recognising her faux pas. 'I assumed…'

Gemma laughed. 'Ha! You actually thought Gary would put his hand in his pocket to buy you a drink! What a laugh!'

'I didn't think that at all! That's why I asked the price.' Kate frowned and pretended to look confused.

Gemma huffed, folded her arms across her ample and extremely exposed chest, and looked away.

Carol caught Kate's eye and grinned. 'You changed your mind… about coming, I mean.'

'Yes. I took your advice. I also thought it might be a good opportunity to meet my future workmates in an informal gathering rather than be thrown in amongst them on my first morning.'

'Good idea. When Gary returns with your drink, we'll mingle. I'll introduce you to some of them.'

'Great! Thanks, Carol.'

'Don't mention it.'

Gary arrived with a round of drinks for his mini harem, as

he called them. When chatter dwindled to nothing and they stood holding their drinks, looking around the room for someone to rescue them, Carol suggested hitting the buffet bar.

The amount of food and the presentation shocked Kate. She was expecting chicken wings, pizza and sausage rolls, not the elegant spread in front of her. Stretching down the long table were turkey and mushroom vol-au-vents, smoked salmon cornets with crabmeat, smoky veggie nachos, pecan shortbreads with blue cheese, and platters of beef, pork and fowl with bowls of crispy salad. Desserts were a selection of cakes, muffins, mini-Christmas cakes, a mountain of mince pies and brandy butter, plus hot Christmas pudding with custard, cream or ice cream. Dotted down the centre of the table were several red Poinsettias decorated with golden stars, mini Santas, elves and fairies.

The group filled their plates and headed off to find a table. It was standing room only, so they squashed around a tiny table littered with empty glasses.

'Here. Hold this,' Gary pushed his plate into Gemma's hand and his drink into Mary's. He opened his fingers and stuck them inside the glasses, lifting them all off the table in one swoop. He lined them up by the wall. The grotto gang stood in silence munching on the tasty fare.

'Ivan seems to be a no-show,' Gemma said, her words laced with spite. 'He must have something better to do. Or someone.' Her eyes flicked in Kate's direction, but Pixie Peppercorn refused to take the bait. '*Ivan* unusual sneaking suspicion he isn't coming,' Gary quipped. A click of Carol's tongue was loud enough for him to hear. 'Gary, that joke's getting rather old now. You've run out of fresh material. Deal with it! Of course Ivan will come. He's the general manager. But unlike us, he'll still be working.' She spied someone in the crowd and called him over. 'Adrian! Just the man I wanted to see.'

'Hello, Carol, how're you doing?'

'Fine, I just wanted to introduce you to Kate. She's joining your marketing team in January.'

Kate shook his hand and scanned his face for first impressions of Carol's news.

'Ah, the famous Kate with the toy collection campaign.' His face broke into a wide smile, and he pumped her arm in an enthusiastic welcome. 'How nice to meet you! That was a great idea, and it blossomed so quickly. Well done! Nice to have you aboard.'

'Thanks,' Kate blushed. 'I'm sure it was more luck than skill.'

'Either way, I'm sure you'll be an asset to our team.' He chatted for a while, then joined his friends.

Carol beamed at Kate. 'There, you see, you've got nothing to worry about. The marketing team are a friendly lot.'

'Thanks for introducing me, Carol. That makes me feel a lot more comfortable about starting in January.'

Gemma slammed her glass down onto the table. 'What? You've wrangled yourself a full-time job here?'

'Yes,' Kate replied.

'Huh! How unfair is that?! I've been trying to get a proper job at Silver Sands for the past three years and you waltz in, open your legs and Ivan delivers.'

'In more ways than one.' Mary giggled.

'Gemma, that's uncalled for,' Carol replied. 'You too, Mary!' 'For your information, I haven't slept with Ivan,' Kate yelled over the music.

Gemma glared at her. 'So that's your secret? You've kept him dangling until he had no other option than to offer you a job.'

Kate grabbed her glass from the table. 'Gemma. Grow up! You

don't know what you're talking about.' Kate needed to get away. She strode away from them, eager to get some space between the group and herself. She wandered through the crowd, suddenly feeling alone and lost.

The buffet table called her name. It no longer resembled the beautifully laid-out fare of earlier. The plates held the remains of food, spilt drinks and overturned glasses that stained the tablecloth. Someone had stolen the beautiful poinsettias. One was on its side. The black soil had cascaded onto an empty plate. Some mince pies still clung together at the end of the table. Kate grabbed one and bit into it. She was savouring the taste when someone grasped her shoulders.

She spun around, clutching the mince pie, expecting to fight; probably with Gemma and shove it in her stupid face.

'Hi!' Ivan smiled down at her. 'Are you enjoying the party?' He spied the mince pie in her clawed fist and hoped he wasn't about to be attacked.

Her whole body relaxed.

Ivan witnessed it. 'Is everything okay?'

Her eyes brimmed with unshed tears. All she wanted to say was, "No. Nothing is right at all," and hurl herself into his arms. But she couldn't.

'Yes,' she replied with the deepest of sighs.

His heart ached to see her so forlorn. His arm wrapped itself around her waist. He pulled her toward him. 'Come with me.'

Once in the office, Ivan sat down on the two-seater sofa and pulled her next to him. Everything overpowered her, and she needed a release. Kate confided in him about Gemma's jealousy. She admitted Mike's vicious revenge was constantly playing on her mind, and she even told him how she and Alison had seen their dad leaving the hippie woman's house.

'I think he's having an affair.'

'Your dad? I doubt that. Haven't you seen the way he looks at your mum? He adores her. That is so obvious. There's no way, he's seeing someone else.'

'Then what was he doing there?'

'I can't answer that, Kate. But I'm sure you'll find out soon enough. Try not to worry.'

She dried her eyes and nodded. 'I hope you're right. It would be out of character for him, that's true.'

Ivan took her hands in his. 'Kate, I hope you know you can come to me with your problems. I'm not speaking in the capacity of your boss. I'm talking to you as your boyfriend.'

Kate's emotions overcame her. She threw herself into his arms and couldn't remember the last time she had felt so safe. 'Thank you.'

'You're welcome. And remember, I'm not going anywhere.' He leaned in and brushed her lips with his.

For Kate, that wasn't enough. She threw her arms around his neck and deepened the kiss until she lost herself in his embrace.

*

On December 22nd Ivan was in his office humming "All I want for Christmas is you," when a knock on the door interrupted his thoughts of him and Kate and their heavy petting session on the sofa the night before.

'Come in!' His voice was light and happy, but his face soon converted into a deep frown and his lips set in a thin line of hatred when he discovered who was in the doorway.

'Mike. What can I do for you?'

The civil servant smiled and sauntered inside. 'I've come to tell you I've been monitoring Kate's movements this morning around the shopping centre, and I have some bad news.'

'Oh, yes?' Ivan tidied his papers on his desk to stop himself from lunging across it and beating Mike to a pulp.

'Yes. She has stolen an item from the drugstore.'

'Really?'

'Yes. But it appears she isn't working alone. She passed the item to her sister, who left the shopping centre and delivered the stolen merchandise to an awaiting car. Her mother was behind the wheel.'

'I see,' Ivan spat from between his teeth. 'I assume you have evidence of this, haven't you? Photographic proof or a video, maybe?'

'Well, I...'

'You must understand, Mike. I can't just take your word for it. That would be like the entire neighbourhood believing Kate didn't pick up after her dog when it was your dog that was to blame.' Ivan enjoyed watching him squirm.

Unnerved, Mike transferred his weight from one foot to the other. 'You don't seem to understand. You can't compare one thing with the other.'

'Yes, I can. You lied about Kate's dog. You told an untruth about her family being in some sort of conspiracy to rob me and the shopping centre. Why should I believe she's stolen something today? You have no proof. And I'll tell you something else.'

'What?'

'You'll never get any, either. Kate's family is cleaner than your reputation or your dogs' backside will ever be. Now, leave my office. I ban you from the shopping centre! If you cause any more upset to Kate or any other member of her family, you can expect to hear from my lawyer.'

Mike's jaw dropped open. 'You intend to take her word over mine? She's a minion, a nothing, working as a silly pixie in a Christmas grotto. I have a degree!'

'Having a university education doesn't mean you are a kind, honest person. Kate is someone who cares so much about others she forgets to think about herself. You are her complete opposite. Goodbye, Mike. I hope I never see you again.'

'We'll see about that!'

'Oh yeah? Then, I recant my last statement. I'll see you in court.'

Mike's face glowed a vivid red. It was more from frustration than embarrassment. 'How dare you!'

'I'll ask you the same question. How dare *you*? I'm warning you. Drop your silly vendetta, or I'll be visiting the job centre and talking to your superiors. Let's see what they have to say about your unprofessional conduct.'

Mike stormed from the office and almost ran down the stairs. But if he thought his humiliation was over, he was mistaken.

When Ivan was sure Mike had gone, he made a quick phone call, grabbed his jacket, and went in search of Kate.

She heard him calling her name above the Christmas music blaring from the grotto. After she had escorted the next family unit into the grotto, she turned to him and smiled.

'Good morning!' She wanted to add "handsome" but thought it was inappropriate under the circumstances. Almost everyone in the queue was watching and listening to the interaction.

Ivan didn't want to wait. He grabbed her arm. 'Carol, I'm taking Kate. Can you cover her spot?'

'Of course, Mr Daniels,' she gushed.

Mary, in the hated Grinch suit, tutted and shook her head.

Gemma folded her arms across her chest. 'Typical!'

Gary jumped to her side and put his arm around her shoulders. 'Don't pout, Gemma. I'll take you out when we've finished, okay?'

Pixie Pumpernickel sniffed. 'All right.'

Gary grinned. The staff Christmas party had been a great opportunity for him to get closer to Gemma. After the amount of alcohol she had chugged down her neck, he had almost had to carry her out to the waiting taxi. He liked his women compliant, but he drew the line at almost catatonic, so being the gentleman he considered himself to be, he didn't take advantage of her. The next morning, he had turned up on her doorstep with a stolen poinsettia plant from the party, surrounded by sprigs of holly and a golden star stuck on the top. He pushed the purloined gift into her arms and asked how she was feeling.

Flabbergasted by his actions, Gemma felt ashamed of her drunkenness the previous night. Her mind flew back to the party. She remembered him putting her in the taxi. She also recalled the kissing and cuddling, which had continued until the taxi came to a stop and the driver informed them with a cough that they had arrived. Gary had walked her to the door, but after that, her mind was a total blank.

The look of concern on his face, that morning when he'd come to check on her, had convinced her of his sincerity. She had asked him inside and, although her head was throbbing, and her mouth felt like the inside of a public toilet; she had nodded and told him she wasn't so bad.

Gary had told her to sit at the kitchen table while he made coffee and toast. She wasn't about to object. The alcohol still swilling around in her stomach made her fight the urge to vomit. But she knew she shouldn't do that in front of Elf Edelweiss. Not if she wanted to keep him interested.

The most embarrassing was yet to come. Her parents came

downstairs still wearing their dressing gowns. They had heard the doorbell and came to investigate.

Gemma cringed while they grilled Gary, as all concerned parents would do. But he soon won them over with his crafty smile and his amusing wit. When they found out he had escorted her home safely, they were his fans for life. He had even got their consent to take her out on Christmas Eve, to a big party in the town centre.

Gemma had to admit she was smitten, too. Now that silly Kate was out of the picture, Gary was all hers, and she wasn't about to let him go without a fight.

*

When they entered "The Duchess" restaurant. Kate smiled, enjoying the opulence and palatial elegance of the decorations.

Ivan approached the maître de. 'Hi, I'm Ivan Daniels. We spoke a while ago.'

The woman's eyes almost laughed. They flicked toward Kate, then back to Ivan. 'Oh, yes! Of course. Please, follow me, sir.'

Kate's annoyance bubbled. She didn't like the interaction between Ivan and the woman. It seemed like they knew each other and were sharing a private joke. Jealousy rose its ugly head, putting Kate on alert.

The maître d' escorted them to a table, gave them two menus, and took their drinks order.   'This is lovely, Ivan, but why now?'

He grinned and held her hand. 'Have you ever had one of those days where you knew everything was going to be better from that day forward?'

She couldn't think of one, but she answered in the affirmative.

His smile broadened. 'That's how I feel.'

Kate monitored him through suspicious eyes. 'What is it you're not telling me?'

'You'll find out soon enough.'

'Ivan, I hate all this suspense.'

He grasped her hand across the table. 'Do you trust me?'

She sighed. 'Yes, but…'

'Then, please, wait a little longer. When we've finished the meal, you will see what I'm talking about.'

Kate smiled but felt sick. Was he about to propose? What would she do if he did? There! In front of all the diners! She'd die of embarrassment.

Her inner voice yelled at her not to be so stupid. Dressed as a pixie every day should make her cringe with shame. Now, that WAS embarrassing! Not this.

Then alarm bells clanged inside her brain. Was she even ready for marriage? It was too soon. They'd only known each other a few minutes, or at least that's what it felt like.

Her heart skipped a beat. What if he didn't propose, and it was something else? Would she be disappointed? She searched her soul and discovered she would. This sensitive man had crawled under her skin and firmly embedded himself inside her heart.

The meal continued, but Kate ate like a sparrow. She was too nervous to tuck into the poached salmon, bechamel sauce, and roasted potatoes with red and green peppers.

Ivan didn't ask if she wanted dessert. He ordered coffee and smiled at Kate's puzzled expression. She could always eat the sweet course whatever the circumstances.

The background music, which was soft enough to talk but loud enough to listen to, halted. A fanfare of trumpets honked through the discreetly positioned speakers.

'Ladies and gentlemen, we have a surprise for one lucky lady sitting with us today.'

Kate cringed. This was it. She knew it. Her nails dug into her palms.

Three servers emerged from the kitchen. One carried a large cake decorated with sparklers fizzing on the top. Another carried a bucket of champagne, and bringing up the rear, was a third who held up a banner with "Congratulations!" emblazoned across it.

Despite the two glasses of wine she had drunk during the meal, and the large coffee, she couldn't swallow! Her throat was as dry as a Jehovah's Witness' birthday party. She glanced at Ivan. He was grinning like the proverbial Cheshire cat.

'Congratulations, Kate Massey. Mr Daniels was the lucky winner of our Mediterranean cruise competition. You will both be seeing in the new year aboard the beautiful cruise liner "Ocean Star" courtesy of Sea-scope Travel.'

The diners cheered and applauded while servers placed the cake and champagne on the table. One reached into her pocket and pulled out an envelope containing the tickets.

Ivan grinned at his date. 'So, what do you say, Kate? Will you go on the cruise with me?'

Overwhelmed with emotion, Kate fought back tears of happiness. Ivan never failed to surprise her, and Alison's bet had changed her life so much, she could hardly believe it.

'YES! Of course!' she said.

The diners cheered and applauded again as Ivan got up, pulled her into his arms and kissed her. Kate no longer cared that the entire restaurant was watching; she revelled being in his embrace.

Chapter Ten

Christmas Day

December 25th

Christmas day began at seven-thirty with the crash and clatter of roasting pans and baking tins. This was Dorothy's usual Christmas morning wake-up call. "I'm up, so you should be too!" was her motto.

Kate heard the floorboards creak outside her room and her dad's familiar pace as he ambled along the corridor, heading for the bathroom.

She hoped he'd hurry! The night before, she had visited Ivan's modern, luxurious home. (Or so it seemed compared to her parents' house.) They had eaten a beautiful meal of garlic prawns cooked in the oven in a bath of Galician Albariño white wine and garlic. Followed by a fruit of the forest cheesecake, which Ivan admitted his mother had made especially for them.

Between copious amounts of wine, they talked about the forthcoming cruise, her new job and their future plans. By the end of the evening, Kate couldn't remember ever feeling so content.

As she snuggled in his arms, he said, 'I'd ask you to stay over, but I wouldn't want your parents to think badly of me.' He nuzzled her neck.

Kate wished he'd posed his words as a closed question so she could have answered in the affirmative. *Yeah, of course I'll stay over. I can't think of a better way of waking up on Christmas morning than wrapped in your arms.* If there was any comeback from her parents, she could (eventually), blame Alison and her bet.

She took the plunge. 'I'll stay. If you want me to.'

Ivan sighed. 'I think we should wait. Once we go on the cruise, I guess everyone will expect something to happen between us. Anyway, it adds to the excitement, don't you think?'

NO! her inner voice screamed. 'Yes,' she stoically replied, despite feeling riddled with disappointment. She could hardly wait to see him undressed. Her mind ran crazy, imagining scenarios of their first time, until she felt dizzy with expectation.

'Come on.' Ivan reached for her hand.

Staring up into his eyes, hoping he had changed his mind, she attempted to look as sultry as possible to convince him to take her to his bed. Or here, right now! On the sofa, on the floor, she didn't care anymore. All she knew for sure was that she longed to be his.

'I'd better take you home,' he said, with a sigh.

Her libido fell quicker than a broken icicle. It pierced her self-esteem like a deadly dagger and melted her raging furnace of a core quicker than being attacked with a bucket of ice-cold water.

*

'KATE!' Dorothy bellowed up the staircase. 'Can you come down and help me and Arthur? Time is flying by and we've so much to do before lunchtime.'

Her daughter groaned. The thought of being bossed around all morning wasn't high on her to-do list. She wanted to stay in bed and dream about Ivan and the upcoming cruise, but experience told her she'd better drag her backside out of bed and get into the kitchen before her mother lost her temper.

'Ah, there you are!' Dorothy said with her forearm stuck inside the scariest-sized turkey Kate had ever seen. Rather than serve their family, it could have fed a small country.

'First, dust the living room, run the vacuum cleaner around and do the same in the dining room. Then set the table for seven.'

A look of confusion spread across Kate's face. 'Seven o'clock?'

'No, silly. Seven people.'

'Who else is coming?'

Dorothy grinned at Arthur. Then turned back to Kate. 'That's a surprise.'

'I hate surprises.'

'Who said it was for you?'

'Can I at least have a coffee first and maybe a piece of toast?'

'Go on then. But don't take all day. We've got a lot to do.'

'I know, Mother!'

Alan appeared in the doorway with Sunday on a lead. 'Morning ladies. Arthur. Merry Christmas, everyone,' he grinned.

Kate couldn't bear to look at him. Last night as Ivan drove her home, she had seen Alan leaving the hippy woman's house again. She hadn't had the chance to confront him without her mum being in earshot, but her mind worked overtime imagining what was going on behind the curtains of number 22.

Her eyes narrowed. Maybe he had popped round with an early Christmas present. Her mind refused to think about what that might be. The thought nauseated her.

He shook Arthur's hand. 'Merry Christmas.'

Arthur tried to control his tears. 'Thank you, Alan. You too.'

Kate cringed when her dad kissed the top of her head.

'Merry Christmas to you, Jellybean.'

She didn't reply.

Alan moved across to his wife. He hugged her and brushed his mouth across her lips. 'Merry Christmas, my love,' he said.

Kate wanted to scream. How could he be so two-faced?

Dorothy extracted her arm from the belly of the turkey and held her hand aloft like she was stopping traffic. 'Merry Christmas to you too. Don't be long this morning, Alan. There's a lot to do.'

He nodded and grinned. 'I know. I'll be quick today.'

His wife sniffed. 'I've heard that before.'

'This time I guarantee it,' he said, flashing her a huge grin.

Sunday pulled on his lead, eager to get outside.

'Come on, my beautiful boy. Let's go for our walk.'

As the front door closed behind him, Kate pondered whether to tell her mother what she suspected. The more she thought about it, the less she could go through with it. If she told her mother now, it would ruin Christmas. She didn't want to be the harbinger of bad news on such an important family day. She would talk to Alison first, and together they would decide what was the best course of action.

Kate took a vicious bite into her slice of toast and a gulp of coffee, but when she felt her mother's eyes boring into her, she pushed back her chair. 'I'm going. I'm going!'

Normally, Kate found dusting cathartic, but today, she couldn't get the images out of her mind of what her father was doing at number twenty-two. She ran the vacuum across the carpets, deep in thought. It was only when her eyes fell on Sunday's dancing feet; Kate realised they had returned, and she was being watched.

Her thumb pushed the off switch, and an uncomfortable silence wedged itself between her and her father.

'Is everything alright, Kate? You seem out of sorts.'

'Yes, everything's fine,' she replied, glad that she couldn't say no.

Alan studied her face, looking for a sign of her true feelings. 'Is everything still okay with Ivan?'

'Huh! Yeah, why shouldn't it be? Just because I've come from a failed relationship doesn't mean to say this one will end up the same way.'

Alan held up his hands in surrender. 'Hey! Don't shoot! I'm only enquiring as to your welfare.'

'I'm fine dad... Are you?'

His face broke into a huge grin. 'Never better!' he said, dancing out of the room.

Sunday followed him out.

Kate clutched the handle of the vacuum cleaner like she wanted to strangle it. This was building up into a nightmare of a Christmas.

In the dining room, she wondered who the extra guest could be. She knew it couldn't be Ivan; he had told her he had plans for Christmas day. She hoped her mum hadn't miscounted and Mike's parents were coming! The thought made her want to crawl under the table and stay there until it was time to leave for the cruise. What if Mike dropped them off and her mum invited him to stay for dinner? Surely, she wouldn't do that! Not after she had heard all the palaver about the dog mess and his allegations that the whole family were thieves.

When the aroma of the hot mince pies filled the room, Kate walked zombie-like into the kitchen.

Dorothy laughed. 'I knew the smell would bring you back.' She turned to Arthur. 'I told you she wouldn't take long to come in here, didn't I?'

Arthur laughed and nodded.

'Here, Kate,' Dorothy said. 'These are for you. Sit down. You should take a break. Mince pies and brandy butter warmed in the microwave, made especially for you.'

Kate peered into her mother's happy face and wanted to cry. The smells and sounds she associated with Christmas overwhelmed her. If her dad was about to ruin all that, she'd never forgive him. If he was having an affair, she'd kill him!

Dorothy frowned. 'Is everything alright, dear?'

'She looks a bit down in the dumps this morning, doesn't she?' Arthur said.

Kate forced a smile. 'Yes, mum. Why wouldn't it be? Wow! These taste delicious!'

'They do, don't they?' Dorothy beamed. She loved nothing more than watching people enjoy her food. She realised Kate had something on her mind, but she also knew her daughter would tell her in her own good time.

*

Alison pulled up at Arthur's house and asked her husband to wait.

'You can help me get him out of the back seat. As you know, it's awkward because his leg is in plaster and then there are the cumbersome crutches.'

'Alright, Alison,' said laid-back James. 'No problem.' He watched his wife walk behind the pensioner.

'How's the leg, Arthur?' she asked, making conversation.

'It's still there. It hasn't dropped off yet, so I guess I'm doing okay.'

Alison laughed. 'That's the spirit. Now, what did you want to get from your house?'

'Some presents.' He opened the front door. 'Would you carry that pile of gifts to the car? Put them on the back seat with me.'

'Yeah, sure.' Alison's forehead creased with confusion. 'Wait, a minute. What have you done? How did you get these? You've been at our house since your accident.'

Arthur grinned. 'I'm not completely useless, you know. I asked my neighbour to get me a few things for you all.'

'You didn't have to do that!'

'It's the least I could do to thank you all for your kindness.'

'It's so nice of you, Arthur. Thank you.'

He nodded and flicked his hand silently telling her it was nothing. 'There's just one small favour I need to ask. Could you drop me in the city centre? I have a minor task I need to do.'

'Yeah, of course.'

'Excellent!' he grinned.

'Anything else, Arthur?'

'Nope. Come on. Let's get going.'

As Arthur hopped down the driveway. James opened the back door and took Arthur's crutches.

'Thank you. That's very kind,' Arthur smiled.

Alison pulled away from the curb and they headed for the town centre.

From the back seat, Arthur directed them to a specific street. As they pulled over and parked, he asked Alison to find some Christmas music on the radio to get them into the right frame of mind. As she fiddled with the stations, he turned to her husband.

'James, my good man, would you be so kind as to post this envelope through that door there?'

'Of course.' He snatched the large manila envelope, jumped out of the car and shoved it through the letter box of the job centre. It landed on top of an envelope embossed with the Silver Springs Shopping Centre logo and another that looked suspiciously like Dorothy Massey's handwriting.

'All done,' James said as he climbed back into the car. 'You're not looking for a job, are you, Arthur?'

'No, but someone I know probably will be soon.'

Alison looked up, saw the job centre and did the maths. 'Arthur, what have you done?'

'Something that should have been done ages ago.'

James looked confused. 'What's going on?'

'I believe Arthur is returning a favour. Isn't that right, Arthur?'

Their eyes locked but brimmed with enjoyment. He had done, what she had been planning to do in the new year.

'Arthur, you never cease to amaze me!' she laughed and shook her head.

'And you, me!' He chuckled. 'Come on. Let's go eat! I'm starving!'

Kate opened the door to Arthur, her sister and James. Again, she wondered who the seventh person could be. Her mum had said the surprise wasn't for her. Sudden fear overcame her. She froze. What if Alison had already told her mother about their suspicions? What if her mother planned to confront Alan, and the seventh person was the woman from number twenty-two? No. surely her mother wouldn't stoop so low as to ruin Christmas for everyone.

Alison shook a bottle of wine and some chocolates in front of Kate's pensive face. 'Hello, earth to Kate, come in, Kate.'

'Huh? What?'

'Can you move out of the doorway so we can all get inside? It's cold out here, you know!'

As Kate stepped aside, James carried in all the presents. Arthur stood grinning, holding onto his two crutches.

'There she is my other guardian angel. Hello Kate,' he grinned.

'Hello again, Arthur.'

Kate told James all about the cruise win as she ushered him and Arthur into the living room and got them a beer. Alan sat down and joined them. They chattered easily as Dorothy gave out final orders to her two girls to prepare for the big meal.

In the kitchen, when the doorbell rang again, Dorothy's eyes sparkled with glee. 'Kate, could you get that, please? My hands are sticky with icing sugar.'

'Yeah,' she said. When she reached the door, her hand faltered at the door-knob. What would she do if the hippie from number twenty-two stood on the doorstep? She took a deep breath and opened the door.

When she saw Ivan, her mouth dropped open. 'Ivan! What are you doing here? I mean, I'm so glad you're here, but how did you...?'

'Your mum invited me. Now close your mouth and invite me in.'

Kate stepped back. 'Yeah, of course!' She couldn't hide her grin. 'When was this all arranged?'

'A while ago. Your mum asked me to come. I couldn't say no. But she vowed me to secrecy. That's why I was a little vague last night when you asked me about *my* plans for today. I couldn't tell you.'

'I'm so happy you're here! This is such a great surprise.' She stood on her tiptoes and kissed him.

'Where should I put these presents?'

'You brought gifts?'

'Of course. It's Christmas.'

'I have a present for you, but I was kinda saving it for the cruise.'

'That's fine. I don't mind waiting.'

Kate pointed toward the living room. 'Please, put them in there under the tree. Can I get you a drink?'

'Yes, a beer would be fine.'

She took him through to the living room and introduced him to Alison, James and Arthur. The latter apologised profusely for his behaviour at the centre.

'Ivan shook his head and flicked his wrist. 'All forgotten. Don't worry about it.'

'And you've already met my dad, Alan.'

'So I have,' Ivan said. 'And Alison too. I believe you interviewed for the job as Pixie Peppercorn. Am I right?'

'Er…'

'It's alright, Alison. He knows. You can tell him the truth,' Kate explained.

Alison had the decency to blush. 'I was doing her a favour. She's useless in interviews.'

'Alison. Please, don't worry. Kate is the best thing that's happened to me in an extremely long time. I'm glad you did it!'

Alison exhaled with relief. 'Thank goodness for that!'

'Cheers!' Arthur said, currently on his third beer.' Merry Christmas everybody!'

'Merry Christmas,' they all said in unison.

Kate grinned. 'I'll bring some canapes.' She hurried to the kitchen where she grabbed her mother by the shoulders and hugged her. 'Thank you, thank you, thank you!'

Dorothy laughed. 'I couldn't think of him sitting in his house alone on Christmas day, and I knew you'd be moping around like a lost soul too, so it made perfect sense to invite him here.'

'So, we could mope together?' Kate joked. 'Mum, you've made my

Christmas.' When her eyes overflowed with tears, Dorothy frowned. 'Then why are you getting upset?'

Kate looked at her mother but couldn't bring herself to tell her about her dad's affair. 'I'm happy, that's all.'

Dorothy turned her daughter toward the door. 'Then go in there and sit with the love of our life. I'll deal with the food.'

Kate kissed her mum and headed into the living room.

'Ah! Here she is, Ivan,' Arthur gushed. 'My guardian angel. She and her sister saved my life, you know.'

'Yes, so I've heard.' He replied. 'Kate is a lifesaver. I can honestly say she's saved mine, too.'

Kate smiled. 'Now, you're pushing it, Ivan.'

'No, I'm not.' He looked around the room. I was in an extremely dark place before Kate came along,' he said to the group. 'I truly believe she came from heaven to save me.'

Alison guffawed. 'Kate the Christmas Angel!'

Kate glared at her.

'I can understand that Ivan,' Arthur replied. 'Both of these girls saved my life and have looked after me ever since. There isn't a lot of compassion in our world these days, but these two girls have it in spades.' He turned to Alan. 'You've done a good job with these two, Alan. They are a credit to you.'

Alison glanced at Kate and rolled her eyes. It was nice to receive such accolades but cringeworthy too.

'Alright, that's enough already,' Alison said. 'Let's go into the dining room and eat!'

Nobody needed telling twice. They followed her into the other room and gasped at the abundance of decorations on the table, the walls and the ceiling.

'You can thank Kate for all this. She did it this morning,' Alison explained, hugging her sister. Everyone took their places and Dorothy emerged from the kitchen carrying the enormous bird.

'Wow! I've never seen such a large specimen!' Arthur said.

His words made the sisters laugh. It sounded so old-fashioned.

Alan stood to do the carving. Everyone watched.

Kate had always felt the carving of the turkey was a type of ritual passed down from generation to generation. She felt overcome with nostalgia. Her eyes sparkled with unshed tears. What if her father ruined it all by running away with the woman at number twenty-two?

More bowls, receptacles, and sauces arrived on the table, and everyone tucked in. The conversation flowed and everyone enjoyed the moment.

After the Christmas pudding and custard, or cheese and crackers for those who preferred a slightly lighter dessert, they all returned to the living room.

'Let's watch the Grinch!' Alison suggested.

'No thanks! Kate replied. It reminded her of Mary, Gemma, Gary and the grotto. She refused to think about the soup of frustration, annoyance and anger she had endured during the last three weeks. 'Let's watch "It's a Wonderful Life."'

'Here, here!' Arthur replied. 'That shows the true spirit of Christmas, not all this modern rubbish.'

Alan nodded his head in agreement. 'Whenever a bell rings, a dolphin gets its fins!'

'Dad!' his daughters groaned.

'Sorry! I mean, whenever a bell rings Kate puts out the bins.'

Everyone laughed.

In the end, it really wouldn't have mattered what film they put on because everyone was soon fast asleep.

Later, when they woke up, Dorothy supplied more drinks and desserts to keep them happy.

'Now, we should open all the presents,' Alan said.

'I'm not sure that's such a good idea, Alan,' Dorothy scowled. 'It's not fair to our guests.'

'Why don't we open one each, Mum?' Kate suggested.

'That's a great idea!' Alan replied. 'I'll be back in a minute.'

Kate and Alison exchanged glances. If their dad disappeared down the garden path, they would never forgive him. They followed his trajectory and realised he was going into the kitchen and out of the back door. They continued to stare at each other until they heard the aged garden shed creak open. Only then did they breathe a sigh of relief.

James handed Alison a small box. She assumed it would contain jewellery, but looked confused when she held up a set of car keys.

'Don't get too excited!' He said, holding up his hands. 'It isn't brand new, but it's a hundred per cent better than that bone rattler you've been riding around in.'

'Where is it?' Alison sat on the edge of her seat, bubbling with excitement.

'It's parked down the street. It's a black Duster. I thought it would help you blend in better when you're out on surveillance.'

'I'm going to see it now!'

'Wait a minute!' Alan had returned with a large, thin package. 'This is for Dorothy, but it concerns you two,' he said, looking at his daughters.

Dorothy held out her arms. 'Ooh! Whatever can it be?'

For the second time, the girls exchanged confused glances.

When Dorothy ripped off the wrapping, she gasped in surprise.

Kate smiled, and Alison frowned.

'This is wonderful, Alan. How did you...?'

'I was at a loss what to get you this year. Then I was looking in the cupboard for something in the living room and on the shelf, I found a photo of the four of us. In the beginning, I was going to ask the painter to replicate the image, but I've grown so fond of Sunday, that I wanted him in the picture. That's why I've been disappearing so often. I've been taking the dog to the painter, so she could add him to the image.'

Kate glanced at Alison. Relief flooded over them. Their father wasn't having an affair!

Dorothy beckoned him toward her so she could kiss him. 'Thank you. That's such a thoughtful gift, Alan.'

He grinned at the girls. 'Do you like it?'

Alison gave him a curt nod.

Kate flashed him a dazzling smile. 'Yes, I love it! And to add Sunday to the painting makes it even more special.'

Their guests expressed their delight at such a delightful gift.

Arthur cleared his throat. 'I've brought some presents for you all. Mostly to thank the girls for helping me in my hour of need. And to you two,' he pointed at Dorothy and Alan. 'You have welcomed me into your home and made me feel so wanted.' His eyes welled with tears. 'This has turned out to be so much better than I imagined Christmas without my wife would ever be.'

Alison passed him a tissue. 'Arthur, I've told you before, we don't allow crying at Christmas! Here,' she pushed a glass of port into his other hand. 'Drink this and eat another piece of Christmas cake.'

Arthur pointed under the tree. 'James, would you mind handing the presents round?'

Dorothy received a hamper full of Christmas delicacies. Alan got a woollen cardigan that he professed to love. Alison and Kate received porcelain figurines of angels. Arthur had paid to have their names and the date they had found him added to the figures.

'You two are my guardian angels and I'll never be able to thank you enough for everything you have done for me!'

'Don't be silly!' Alison replied. 'The presents are beautiful. Thank you very much, but anyone would have done the same thing if they had been in the same situation.'

'I'd like to agree with you, but I can't. Especially when I shouted at Kate and Alan for something they hadn't done!' He glanced sheepishly at Kate. 'I also doubt everyone would have continued to look after me and invite me to their house for Christmas. This is the least I could do to say thank you.'

Alison patted his arm. 'We've officially adopted you now, so you better get used to this!'

When more tears fell, she handed him a tissue.

'My turn,' Ivan said. He handed Kate a long, thin, red velvet box. 'What's this? You are taking me on a cruise. That's my present.' 'Yes, but you knew about that. I wanted to get you a surprise gift.' She studied the box, running her hand over the top of the velvet. 'Open it, Kate!' Dorothy said. 'We all want to see what you've got.'

Kate removed the lid. Inside was a gold St. Christopher on a chain. She gasped. 'Ivan. It's beautiful. Thank you!'

'What a thoughtful gift!' Dorothy said, smiling at Ivan.

He took the smile and passed it to Kate. 'I thought if we are going to travel, you might appreciate it.'

Kate got up and kissed him lightly on the lips. 'I love it! Thank you so much.'

Chapter Eleven

The Cruise

On December 30th Ivan and Kate stood on the dock in Barcelona, shading their eyes from the afternoon sunshine. The warmth seeped into their skin and filled them with a level of calmness they couldn't quite explain. They shuffled forward in a long line of passengers all waiting to take their first steps aboard the Ocean Star cruise liner. Kate was so excited, she couldn't keep still. Her chattering had become incessant.

Ivan nodded and grinned. He loved how she saw the world through a child's eyes, and he revelled in her enthusiasm.

They inched closer and closer to the gangplank. Ivan clutching the tickets with one hand and Kate's hand in the other. Once they got on board, he pulled her over to the ship's railings.

'What a fantastic city this is! We should come back one day to explore it with more time.'

Kate nodded, then looked away. Her eyes filled with tears.

'What's wrong?'

'Nothing. I was thinking about my family. When they said goodbye at the airport, I felt so sad leaving them. We've always spent the New Year together. We've never missed one yet. It's true, Alison and I would go out after midnight, but we were always together as a family when Big Ben chimed, announcing the new year.'

Ivan rubbed her shoulders. 'We don't have to go if you don't want to. I can take you back home.'

'No! Don't be silly. This is the opportunity of a lifetime. I realise that. Don't worry about me. I'll be fine.'

'Are you sure?'

'I'm positive.'

'Come on. Let's go find our cabin.'

Kate wiped her eyes, took Ivan's hand and walked inside the enormous cruise liner. Her eyes grew wide with the opulence on board. Everywhere gleamed sparkled and shone.

Ivan accepted a leaflet from a member of the crew and as they walked, he read about all the facilities on board. 'There's a casino, a theatre a ballroom and a disco. They have four different restaurants with a variety of cuisines available. There's a cinema, three swimming pools, a fitness centre – probably to work off all that food. Oh, they've also got a spa and a salon. There's a full programme of entertainment and different excursions ashore almost every day! This sounds great!'

Kate forced herself to smile. She had agreed to come on the cruise. She was with the man she loved, so there was no reason to be melancholy. 'Sounds like we're going to have a lot of fun!' she said. 'But this ship is like a maze. If we don't find our cabin soon, we may end up sleeping in a lifeboat like a couple of stowaways.'

Ivan bent his head and kissed her. 'As long as I'm with you, I'd be happy anywhere.'

Kate stared into his eyes. His love for her radiated from them, and she felt strangely humbled that he had chosen her.

As they pulled apart, a steward appeared beside them.

'Can I help you folks? You look kinda lost.'

'Yes, please,' Kate replied, not forgetting her bet with Alison still hadn't finished.

'It is all confusing at first, but you'll get the hang of it.' He glanced at the tag on their room key. 'At least you are on the right deck. That's a good start. Now, if you'd both like to follow me, I'll take you to your door.'   Once inside their cabin, Kate stood beside the double bed, taking in the opulent surroundings. It wasn't a huge space, but it was decorated with top-class fixtures and fittings. She stared out of the porthole. All she could see were the undulating waves of the wintery Spanish coastline. She found it hard to believe they would soon be at high sea and heading toward their next destination.

Ivan checked all their luggage had arrived, tipped the steward, then sat on the bed, bouncing up and down to test it. 'It's a good sturdy mattress,' he said, then wished he hadn't. It sounded suggestive, and he hadn't thought it through.

Kate turned. Ivan saw her vulnerability etched across her face. He held out his arm and beckoned her to come closer.

'Kate, don't look so worried. We'll take this at your pace, okay? You set the rules.'

She nodded, then mouthed yes, for Alison's sake. She was annoyed with herself. What was wrong with her? On Christmas Eve, she would have readily jumped into his bed and ravaged his body. Today, she was shy and riddled with nerves. It made little sense!

'I don't know what's wrong with me!' she said. 'I'm sorry.'

'Stop apologising! I'm happy to be with you. This is a special trip and I want you to enjoy it.' He stood up, believing she would feel less nervous if he wasn't on the bed. 'How about we unpack, then go explore?'

Kate nodded. Ivan's words had helped instil within her a feeling of control. The ball was in her court, as her dad liked to say. As she unpacked, she found her present to Ivan. She gripped the package between her fingers, trying to decide what to do.

'Ivan? This is for you.' She couldn't look at him as she passed it over.

'Thank you,' he said.

Confused by her lack of eye contact, he sat on the nearest chair. When he opened the package, a babydoll nightdress with matching panties fell onto his lap. Following the Christmas theme, it was red and edged with white marabou fur.

'I wanted to give you these now, so you know I am prepared to do this, Ivan.' Her eyes dropped to the carpet. 'But I need a bit of time.'

Ivan couldn't find words to reply. One part of his anatomy had already responded, and he was glad the wrapping paper on his lap was covering it pretty well. He didn't answer until she looked at him.

'Thank you, Kate, that means a lot.'

She took his hand. 'Come on. Forget the unpacking. Let's go explore!'

'Great!' he replied. His hands tried unsuccessfully to hide the bulge in his trousers. 'Let me pop to the bathroom first.'

That evening, they sat in their chosen dining room and stared at the enormous display of food laid out for the evening buffet. Kate grasped her knife and fork in her fists and pretended to bang them on the table. 'Bring me food! Bring me food!'

Ivan laughed and laid an arm across hers to stop her actions. 'It's a buffet, you crazy person. We help ourselves to the food!'

'I know!' She forced a laugh. She was only acting the fool to break the awkward silence that had fallen around them.

Her eyes perused the room. It was more than half full of diners who, she realised, were all eating. 'I think we should head to one end of the buffet table and look for a plate to pile food onto it. Have you seen the size of the portions some of these diners have got? They'll go up two dress sizes if they continue eating like that!'

Ivan laughed. 'Trust you to notice something like that.'

'What's that supposed to mean? You can't miss those mountains of food!'

Ivan stood up. 'Lead the way, Pixie Peppercorn.' He held out his hand to help her up.

'Hey! I hope you weren't expecting me to have brought my costume because I left that firmly sealed inside my locker at work!'

'Oh, no. Really?'

Kate nodded.

'Huh! Then I suppose the sexy Santa ensemble will have to suffice!'

Kate grinned, despite her nervousness for that evening.

*

After dinner, they spent the next few hours in the ballroom watching the on board entertainment. To open the show was a small group of dancers wearing light purple feather headdresses and matching boas, sparkling silver bikinis, fishnet tights and silver high-heeled shoes. They performed in between three main acts: a singer, a ventriloquist and a comedian.

Ivan and Kate partook of a few drinks and were both feeling in that happy-drunk stage by the time they wandered back to their cabin.

The alcohol had infused Kate with a false sense of empowerment. She snatched up the babydoll nightie. 'I'll be back in a minute,' she gabbled, then locked herself in the tiny bathroom.

Ivan froze, overcome with indecision. Should he get undressed and climb under the covers, or would Kate find that presumptuous? He looked around the cabin for inspiration. His eyes fell on his phone. He turned it on and searched his playlist for Christmas pop songs.

He turned the sound up, then lowered it, then turned it up again. Ivan was also feeling unnerved. He hadn't slept with another woman since his marriage to his wife. And since her death, he hadn't even contemplated finding release in the arms of anyone else. But then Kate had come along and knocked him off his feet. He had genuine feelings for her and didn't want to blow it by doing something wrong. What if he couldn't please her in bed? He worried her ex might have been some sort of sex god and he, Ivan, would be left floundering on the sidelines. She might even consider throwing him overboard! On impulse, he swallowed his nerves, undressed down to his underwear then slid under the cool cotton sheets.

Kate scrutinised herself in the bathroom mirror. She looked good in the nightie, but, even with the copious amounts of alcohol she had imbibed for courage, she worried her performance wouldn't match up to his deceased wife. She ran a brush through her knotted hair, touched up what was left of her make-up, took a deep breath, and stepped outside.

Mariah Carey belted out, "All I want for Christmas is you," and Kate swayed, singing along to the lyrics. Not as easy as she imagined it would be in her happy-drunk stage and with the undulating waves that rocked the ship from side to side.

Her impromptu dance, rather than turning Ivan on, made him smile. She looked so cute and childlike that it almost seemed indecent to think she was about to get into his bed. He had to remind himself she was an adult. A consenting one! And she was doing this because she wanted to.

At the bottom of the bed, she crawled on all fours along the eiderdown and up the bed toward him. He tried to swallow, but his Adam's Apple refused to obey him. All he could do was pull back the covers and invite her inside.

'Are you sure you want to do this?' he asked, his voice almost a whisper.

'YES!' she replied with much more forced enthusiasm than she felt. Her teeth were almost chattering with nervousness. Neither of them should have worried. They were perfect for each other.

'Come here,' he said…

*

The following morning, December 31st, they awoke in each other's arms.

Ivan kissed her forehead. 'Good morning, Beautiful. How are you?'

She wanted to say her nether regions felt like they'd been attacked by a cheese grater, her mouth felt like a rodent had crawled inside and died, and she had the mother of all headaches, but she held her tongue. 'Fine,' she said with a shy smile.

Their lovemaking had been intense and pleasurable, better than both of them had expected. She didn't want to say anything detrimental and fill him with doubt. She left the smile lingering there on her lips and hoped she looked happy and dreamy.

'Yes, I'm feeling great! And you?'

He returned the facial expression. 'Never been better. Are you sure you're alright? I wasn't too rough, was I?'

She cringed, still thinking of the deal with her sister. She couldn't wait for the day to be over so she could answer however she wanted. 'Yes. BUT...' her voice rose, not wanting him to interrupt. '...It was fine. I mean great! It was perfect. I was nervous, but...'

'So was I!'

'You?'

'Yeah. It's been a long time since I... well, you know. I didn't know if I'd be up to your standards.'

Kate ran a finger down his stubbly chin. 'You were even better than I hoped you'd be.'

He frowned. 'Should I take that as a compliment?'

'Yes, of course!'

'Okay then. Come here. I have a sneaking suspicion we might be late for breakfast this morning.'

*

The cruise ship had docked in Malaga during the night and there was an excursion planned to the town centre at midday.

Kate wanted to stay on board and do a different type of excursion- of Ivan's body- but he had insisted they join the stream of passengers walking down the gangplank to the port.

She felt slightly niggled that he would prefer to wander around a city rather than stay in the cabin with her and make love. After all, they had waited quite some time to consummate their relationship and now she'd done it; she wanted to do it again. And again, and again!

Plastering on a smile, she held his hand. He had won the trip. The least she could do was to look happy.

The excursion around Malaga was better than she had expected. A guide took the group around the Alcazaba, an old Spanish fortress. They visited the Roman theatre, then stopped for a gorgeous lunch off the main square. Later, they wandered around the impressive Picasso Museum and then visited the apartment, where he grew up. After a visit to the Cathedral of Encarnación, they made their way back to the bus. It was almost six o'clock in the afternoon by the time they returned to the ship.

Back on board, Ivan suggested they freshen up, then have a quick drink in a bar because the New Year's Eve gourmet dinner wouldn't start until nine o'clock that night.

Once again, Kate felt almost rejected. She had hoped for a lie down that would end in a passionate reunion, but Ivan appeared nervous and distracted. She wondered if his words that morning were all a sham and she had been a major disappointment in the bedroom.

'You go in the shower first,' he said. 'I'll wait.'

But he hadn't waited. When she had soaped up her body and was washing her hair. She heard him shout through the building steam.

'Kate? I'm popping out for a minute. I won't be long.'

He didn't give her the chance to reply. She heard the cabin door slam shut, and he was gone.

Alone in the cabin, she glanced at the bed and wondered if she should slide under the fresh covers and wait for him. Should she wear the Santa nightie again? Would that turn him on, or would she look desperate like some sex-starved addict? Kate frowned. She was overthinking this.

Wearing a light blue summer dress, she styled her hair, then sat on the bed reading a book. But it was impossible to concentrate. Her morale dropped. She missed her family.

Then she remembered the ship was still in port. She should have a signal on her phone. If she could speak to her mum, she'd feel much better.

Kate punched in the home number and waited. The phone rang and rang. Not speaking to them only highlighted her loneliness. Tears pricked the backs of her eyes, but when she heard the cabin door opening, she hid the phone under her pillow, sniffed and shook herself, hoping to look bright and cheerful.

When Ivan burst in, his eyes were alight with amusement. 'Oh, you're there. Sorry I took so long. I got talking to some people and I couldn't get away.'

'Who were they?'

'Just other guests who are looking forward to this evening's New Year celebrations. They have agreed to join us for dinner this evening.'

'Great!' she said with forced enthusiasm. She couldn't understand his excitement at seeing in the New Year with strangers.

'Are you ready to go?' He said, breaking into her thoughts. 'We could sit in the bar with the huge windows and watch Malaga getting smaller and smaller as the ship leaves port.'

'Yes,' she said, sticking to the rules of her agreement with Alison, while a longing to speak to her family ate her up inside.

*

The restaurant was buzzing by the time they arrived. They sat at a table set for seven people and Kate wondered if she'd like the strangers Ivan had forced upon her. She also hoped she wouldn't tear up and burst into tears when the clock struck twelve and she wasn't with her family.

Ivan witnessed her reticence. 'Is everything alright, Kate? You're extremely quiet this evening.'

She fiddled with her microphone necklace. 'Yes.'

'Everything will be fine. Just you wait and see.'

She didn't want to dampen his enthusiasm. He was giddy with excitement, but she felt about as festive as a week-old Brussel sprout.

Her eyes perused the beautifully decorated room. A small group of musicians, ensconced in a corner, played a selection of upbeat Christmas pieces with a personal jazzy twist. A young woman crooned into the microphone and smiled at the guests. Servers scurried from one place to another, delivering trays of drinks and at the far side, other waitresses brought out the first course.

'If they don't hurry up, they'll miss the aperitifs,' Kate said.

Ivan cupped her chin in his hand and grinned. 'They'll be here. Don't worry.' He drew her towards him and kissed her.

As she felt her whole body react, he abruptly pulled away.

'Here they are now!' he said, pointing to the main door behind her.

Once again, Kate felt deflated. What was wrong with him? Why would he care more about a bunch of strangers arriving on time than kissing her? Sighing, she plastered on a smile to meet his new friends.

When she turned, her mouth hung open in shock!

'Surprise!' The group said in unison, then they burst into laughter.

'Mum? Dad?' She stared at Alison, James and Arthur! 'I don't believe it. How did you…? When did you…?'

They each took their turn to hug her and shake Ivan's hand.

'We'll let your boyfriend explain,' Alan said, patting Ivan on his shoulder.

Kate stared at him, with tears of joy falling down her cheeks. 'How did you do this?'

I paid for your parents to come because I knew how much you

would want them to be here for the new year. Alison and James insisted on paying for themselves.

'Yeah,' Alison replied. 'Then we couldn't leave poor old Arthur at home on his own, especially since we adopted him, so we all chipped in and paid for his ticket, too.'

Kate sank into her chair as they all took theirs.

'I can't believe it! This is so great!' She turned to Ivan. 'How did you keep this a secret? When did they arrive?'

'This morning. That's why I wanted us to go on the excursion. Otherwise, they would have had to stay trapped in their cabins all day so as not to bump into you.'

'So, these are the so-called strangers you met while I was in the shower!'

Ivan held up his hands. 'Guilty as charged. Finally, I can tell you the truth!' he said with a contrived sigh.

Alison fiddled with her wine glass. 'Yeah, talking about telling the truth. Kate, I have a confession to make.'

Her sister frowned. 'Alison, I don't like the sound of this.'

'You know our agreement...?'

'Yeah. Don't you dare back out, now, Alison. I've stuck to my end of the bargain!'

Alison held up her hands in surrender. 'Listen. I still intend to pay for you to go to university or to get a flat whatever you want, but the thing is, there is something that I didn't tell you.'

Kate's eyes narrowed. Her body tensed. 'What is it?' she replied, cringing with nervous tension.

Alison refused to make eye contact. She took a long, deep breath in. 'Uff. Okay. Here goes. Kate, there never was a microphone. I didn't listen in to your conversations. Not a single one.'

Kate's mouth dropped open again. 'What?'

'The necklace you have been wearing all this time is my Christmas present to you. Go on. Look inside.'

Confused, Kate grasped the pendant and clicked it open. She gasped. 'It's the same as the photo dad had painted for mum, but minus the dog.'

Alan coughed. 'Yeah. I got a telling-off from your sister about that. You see, it was her who had left the photograph I found in the drawer. I sort of spoiled her surprise by duplicating it for your mum. Here.' He shoved a tiny painting in her hand. 'Once Alison told me about her gift to you, I went to ask the painter if she would do a tiny portrait of Sunday, too, so you can add it to your locket.'

Kate cradled the image in her palm. 'Thanks, Dad. It's beautiful.' She turned to face her sister. 'But, Alison, you mean to tell me I've been saying yes for almost an entire month, and you never heard a single word?'

Her sister had the decency to look ashamed. She nodded. 'I wanted to force you to come out of your shell, step out of your comfort zone and experience a bit of life.'

Kate wanted to be angry, but she couldn't be.

'Do you forgive me?' Alison asked.

Kate grabbed her sister and hugged her. When she pulled away, both had tears in their eyes.

'YES! How can I be angry, Alison? Look what has happened to me. I've met the man of my dreams, got a full-time job which I know I'll love, and I get to spend the new year on this cruise in the Mediterranean Sea with all of you! Alison, I can't thank you enough. And I love the locket. Thank you so much!'

The sisters embraced again and the rest of the group applauded.

'Great,' Alison said. 'Then, as of this moment, I release you from our deal. You no longer have to say yes to everything. Only if you want to, of course.'

'Thank you.' Kate turned to Ivan. 'As for you. I didn't know you could be so sneaky! But thank you for arranging all of this. It means the world to me.'

Ivan folded her into his arms. 'You are welcome.'

Arthur extracted a huge cotton handkerchief to wipe his eyes and blow his nose. 'I've said it before, and I'll say it again. These two girls are my guardian angels. They deserve the very best.'

'Don't you dare start crying again, Arthur!' Alison said.

'I agree with Arthur,' Ivan replied, pulling Kate away from him. 'They are both exceptional women. He stared into her eyes. 'Now, Kate, I only have one more question to ask you,' he said. 'And I'm going to need witnesses.'

Kate could hardly breathe. Words disintegrated behind her lips. Her brain turned to fuzz. She could only nod in response.

'Kate. As Arthur said, I believe you are an angel in disguise. You came to save me from myself.'

She shook her head. 'I'm no...'

Ivan placed a finger on her lips to silence her. 'I only have one more question for you, Kate.' He dropped to one knee and held out an engagement ring. 'Will you marry me?'

Tears coursed down her cheeks. Her heart was so full, she thought it would burst. For the first time since her ordeal had begun, she was free to give her honest opinion.

'YES!' she said. 'Of course, I will!'

The restaurant erupted with applause. Cheers and shouts of congratulations echoed all around them.

Ivan kissed her so passionately their hearts beat as one. Kate melted into his arms and knew she'd stay there forever.

THE END

'

REVIEWS

As a struggling writer,

I humbly ask of you,

To spare just a minute, please

And leave a short review.

Every comment written,

And every five-star rating

Helps me as a writer,

And is a cause for celebrating.

So, help a struggling author,

As then, my friend, you see,

What may seem unimportant,

Will mean the world to me.

I'd like to say a huge thank you to **Danny Marquez**, who always reads my books and finds my silly mistakes. Muchísimas Gracias, amigo!

If you enjoyed 'Say Yes to Everything at Christmas', you may like to try 'An Education for Emma' another Romantic comedy. Here is the Blurb and first chapter.

Blurb: for **'An Education for Emma.'**

Emma Graham believes her bad luck has changed for the better when she lands a new job as a primary school teacher. But when her ex-boyfriend, Chris, stalks the school perimeter, and Emma's new love interest, Dominic, appears to be hiding a dark secret, her life soon spins out of control.

To make matters worse, the headmistress throws her together with the new P.E. teacher, Phil, who has a secret crush on her. They have to organise the school Christmas concert together, with hordes of six-year-olds and pushy parents, which only adds to her troubles.

Determined to find out what Dominic is hiding, Emma coerces her best friend Sue, and the P.E. teacher to help her discover the truth, with a series of comical results.

All comes to a head at the school Christmas concert when the three men come face to face and give a whole new meaning to Christmas Punch! But who will win her heart? And who will ruin Christmas?

Emma may be the teacher, but she's the one who receives an education… in love, deceit and infatuation.

Chapter One

First day of school

No one paid the slightest attention to the slim young woman blocking the imposing school entrance. Sleep-deprived parents were too busy coaxing the least enthusiastic of their offspring through the main gates.

Emma was vaguely aware of the amalgam of brightly dressed midgets barging past her; some laughing and chattering, others crying or taking tantrums, while she stood frozen to the spot. Her tongue stuck to the roof of her mouth as fear overtook her. Her hand closed around the acceptance letter as she perused the grandiose school building; taking in every aspect. The myriad of classroom windows blinked back at her like sets of inquisitive eyes in the weak, unexpected September sunshine.

Emma lowered her gaze. She noticed two adults standing at the main door, welcoming the noisy rabble inside. The elder of the two lifted one hand, shielding her eyes from the weak September sun. Her action seemed exaggerated, as though she wanted to draw attention to the fact Emma was in her sights.

Aware she was under suspicion, Emma swallowed. She edged forward into the rabble and ruckus, her long legs tottering on new high-heeled shoes, and quite unsuitable. A mini tornado of pattering feet and jiggling schoolbags hankered her trajectory. She strode towards the teacher in what she hoped was a determined manner.

Six steps into her pilgrimage, one of the older children goose-stepped in front of her. His backpack swung into her hip, knocking her off balance. One second, she was tall and erect, the next she fell in a jumbled heap of arms and legs onto the playground tarmac. Her once coiffured long blond hair hung in thick strands over her face like melted stringy cheese. The previous riotous din fell quiet, frozen in time. The children shuffled shoulder to shoulder, forming a wobbly circle around her. From her prone position, they reminded her of a pack of hungry hyenas, about to pick over her bones.

'Miss, there's a woman on the floor here.' The kid who had caused the calamity shouted so loudly, the whole school and most of the surrounding area heard his announcement.

Emma cringed, wishing the floor would swallow her up quicker than the hungry hyenas were threatening to do. She kept her eyes cast downwards, then noticed with rising horror she had ripped her nylon tights–also new and bought for the occasion. She now sported a great big hole at the knee. Her bleeding kneecap was permeating the thin nylons and creating a rivulet of blood down her shin.

Shit! I look like a primary school student, rather than a teacher! She thought as the hyenas parted and a pair of size six, brown, laced brogues came into her periphery.

'Oh, dear, oh dear, oh dear!'

Emma traversed the length of the shoe owner's body. She took in the thick nylon support stockings, a beige two-piece suit, which trapped two ample breasts, and grey hair scraped back into a tight bun. For a moment, she wondered if by falling; she had somehow been flung through time and had landed on the film set of a Miss Marple mystery. Emma tried to assess the mood of the face, scowling down at her. The woman's face hinted at a smile that confused her even more.

'What's happened here, then?'

Her question revoked Emma's theory of a murder mystery detective. She resisted the urge to say that little hooligan knocked me flying! Emma swallowed. Debilitated and frightened, she knew if she opened her mouth, she'd burst into tears, so she refrained from replying. With a wobbly finger, she pointed to her ripped tights, bleeding knee and scuffed suede shoes.

The teacher leaned forward to examine the damage, and Emma regressed to her childhood. For a second, she thought the woman was going to kiss her knee better.

It didn't happen.

'That's a nasty fall you've had there.' She eyed Emma with suspicion. 'What are you doing here? Can I help you?'

Emma, still unable to trust opening her mouth without bursting into tears, held out her crumpled letter with a shaky hand.

The woman perused the correspondence and realisation kicked in. 'Ah! Of course, the new substitute teacher. Oh, dear! What a bad beginning you're having.'

Emma nodded, wondering if the woman meant to sound so condescending or if she was so used to talking to the youngsters that way it was second nature to her. What a predicament to get yourself in, she chastised herself.

The teacher held out her hand.

Emma faltered; unsure whether it was a gesture of welcome, or leverage to haul herself back onto her feet. The first option seemed the most likely, so she gave the proffered extremity a solemn shake. 'How do you do?'

'Oh!'

The older woman's exclamation forced Emma to admit she had made yet another faux par and should have got to her feet. She grappled on the ground and heaved herself up onto two tentative legs.

The elder female furrowed her brow, unable to decipher the dishevelled young woman. 'Well, I'm Mrs, Beecham, I'm the head teacher here, nice to meet you.' Then, realising she had an audience of nosey students, she clapped her hands together. 'Come on, girls and boys. Hurry now. Get to class!'

Emma remained standing on wobbly legs just as one heel of her ruined new shoes separated from the sole with a snap. She lurched and stumbled sideways, reaching out for the headmistress and almost pulling her down towards the tarmac with her.

'Dear, oh dear, oh dear!' Mrs Beecham shook her head; clicked her tongue and helped her up again. 'I think I'd better take you to the staff room so you can sort yourself out a little before you meet your class.' She turned her back on Emma, expecting her to follow, then strode towards the main entrance.

Emma lolloped behind the headmistress, the broken shoe

forcing her to walk on the ball of her foot. The bleeding kneecap on the other leg made her wince in pain with every step. She swung her arms at either side in an ungainly fashion, trying to keep her balance.

'Look, that woman walks like an orang-utan!' she heard one child shout.

The hyenas erupted into laughter as Emma blushed a deep crimson and hobbled towards the doors.

***

Emma's embarrassment rose even further on entering the staff room. All eyes fell on the dishevelled individual who wished she could either disappear or turn back time and start the day again. Only this time, she'd wear trousers and flat shoes that couldn't possibly get her into any trouble.

The bell rang. A shrill triple-beeping sound forced most of the teachers to gather their books, bags and papers together and head for the door. They nodded with amused interest as they passed. Each nod aided in raising Emma's embarrassment level another notch.

Mrs Beecham looked around at the few remaining staff members, trying to decide whom she could dump Emma on and rid herself of the problem.

'Ah, Daisy, be a dear and help me, could you? This is…' she glanced at the crumpled letter, 'Emma Graham. She's the substitute teacher for Janice Jones. Emma's had a bit of an accident in the playground. Could you sort her out for me?' She gave Emma a slight push towards the bemused woman. 'I'll come back in about fifteen minutes. Thanks a lot.' Beecham turned. 'Welcome to Saint Jude's, dear,' she patted her on the shoulder, then fled out of the staffroom as if the hem of her skirt was on fire.

Daisy stood by the coffee machine, mug in hand. She stirred her drink and perused Emma's dishevelled state with a hint of amusement.

'Jesus! What the hell happened to you?'

'I got ambushed by one kid and his backpack.'

'Ah! Lethal things, backpacks… and kids too, come to think of it!' She grinned. 'Here, sit down, have my coffee. You look like you need it more than me.'

Emma lowered herself to the nearest sofa and took the mug with a grateful smile. 'Thanks.'

'So, what did you do to deserve this?' Daisy curled her lip in disgust and swung her arm around the staffroom, as though she were presenting her domain.

Emma's life flashed before her. Unhappy with her job in a supermarket, she had studied for an Online Degree. It was during that time, she discovered her boyfriend, Chris, had slept with their boss, Sara, a high school classmate of Emma's. That had only added insult to injury. Emma had thrown Chris out, quit her job and started work in a little bookshop. The pay wasn't great, but she was free from work gossip and loved having access to all those books.

Daisy stared at her, waiting for an answer, but Emma had no intention of divulging her private life to a stranger.

'I'm not exactly sure. The school board rang, and I took them up on the offer,' she said.

'Good for you!' Daisy plonked herself on the sofa next to Emma with a fresh cup of coffee. 'The woman you're replacing, Janice, is up the spout.' She registered Emma's confusion and extrapolated. 'She's only about two months along, but Mrs Beecham wants her out of here as soon as possible.'

'Why?'

Daisy's voice dropped to a conspiratorial whisper. 'Well, Janice isn't married, you see. And, as this is a Catholic school, it's like a cardinal sin or something. Mrs Beecham would prefer her to be off the premises before her bump shows.'

'Oh, I see.' Emma cupped her hands around the coffee mug and took a grateful swig.

Daisy stood up. 'I guess I'd better sort your knee out.' She peered at the now congealed blood. 'That looks painful.' She shook her head. 'Kids these days have no respect. Bloody little hooligans!'

Stunned, a teacher would refer to children in such a way, Emma was lost for words.

'There was a time when teachers were revered,' Daisy continued. 'Now we're like glorified babysitters. Sometimes, I think some parents don't care less about the academic prowess of their kids. They just want them out of their hair for a few hours. A terrible state of affairs.'

'I'm sure they're not all like that,' Emma said.

'No, not all of them.'

'So why do you do it?'

Daisy stared into space. 'Because, if I'm being honest, I love the little mites. Well… most of them, anyway.'

***

Emma set off down the corridor, with Mrs Beecham by her side to meet her new class. She tried to hide her uneasiness, but was more nervous than she cared to admit. Her fear of the unknown was making her jittery, and when she looked down and witnessed the sorry state she was in, she cringed with embarrassment. Her ripped tights had been relegated to the wastepaper bin in the staff room. Daisy had botched together her broken heel with half a roll of sticky tape. She had further embellished her handiwork by wrapping layer after layer of it around Emma's ankle to keep the shoe in place. To add insult to injury, on her bust knee, Emma sported a huge, 'Sponge Bob Square Pants' plaster.

Mrs Beecham eyed the spectacle, screwing up her face in mild disgust, but realising Daisy had done the best she could under the circumstances, she kept mum.

The head stopped outside a bright purple door. "We are all little stars!" was scrawled across it. Below were a host of shiny gold examples. Each with a child's name written across it.

'Here we are. This is you.' Mrs Beecham knocked on the classroom door, opened it and, seconds later, Emma became the centre of attention.

The teacher sitting at her desk made a swooping assessment from Emma's head to her broken shoes in seconds. Thirty-two little heads swung towards the door. Sixty-four inquisitive eyes, belonging to a class of nosey six-year-olds, scrutinised the stranger in their midst. A few giggled and pointed at the plaster, others gawped at the sticky-taped shoe. Everyone waited with building excitement to find out why the strange, beaten-up woman was in their midst.

'Good morning, Mrs Beecham and God bless you,' they chanted.

Mrs Beecham nodded in their direction. 'Good morning, children... Ah, er... Janice,' she pronounced her name as if she had a bad smell up her nose. 'This is Emma Graham; she will substitute you.'

Janice peered past the head teacher. 'Oh, that's great!' she said, beaming at Emma, and recognising her real life ticket to salvation. Her "get out of jail free" card.

Mrs Beecham scarpered as though the mere thought of being in a classroom of mini-humans was repulsive, leaving Emma to fend for herself. 'What happened to you?' Janice stared in surprise at the bloody dishevelled mess before her as Mrs Beecham disappeared down the corridor.

'I got knocked down in the playground,' Emma said, feeling like a kid again.

'Oh, dear!'

Emma wondered if those two words were the school's catchphrase.

'Well, you can't work in broken high-heels. Here, try these on.' Janice shoved a pair of flat slip-on shoes into Emma's hands. 'You might be a bit more comfortable. I have two pairs. I alternate between them during the day. It seems to stop my ankles from swelling.'

Emma took the shoes and cast a grateful smile in Janice's direction. 'Thank you! But won't you need them yourself?'

Janice wafted a hand to trivialise the situation. 'Nah! One day won't matter.' She wandered away to answer a student's question, so Emma sat on the teacher's chair and tried to remove the sticky tape without yelping. It was stuck fast to her skin. Each gentle tug was ripping her hair out, reminding her of a painful wax treatment. She tried pulling it, which only prolonged the agony.

'Miss. You should pull it off in one go. That's what my dad told me. It hurts. But not so much.'

Emma looked up. Four students leaned over their desks, watching her.

'Yeah, my dad said that too.'

'My mum told me.'

'Okay, okay,' Emma snapped. 'I'll take your advice.' She grabbed hold of the remaining tape with both hands and ripped it off in one dramatic swoop, biting into her lip to stop herself from yelping.

'That's a good girl,' she heard one of them say. The others gave her a round of applause.

'We should kiss it better now. That's what my mummy always does.'

'Yeah? Mine too. Ha!'

'And mine!' They giggled at the similarity, then turned to face Janice. 'Miss... Can we kiss...?'

'No!' Janice's voice reverberated around the classroom. 'Leave Miss Graham alone. Get on with your work, please!'

Emma spent the morning taking notes. Janice detailed the children's progress and divided them into two groups: the motivated and the intelligent. Then came the average students. Those who liked some subjects and hated others. And finally, those, who - in Janice's own words - were little horrors whom she despised with a passion.

'They've no respect, don't want to be here, and make it impossible for those students who want to learn.'

Lost for words, Emma stared at her, tilting her head upward in a sign of recognition. This seemingly placid person has a dark side. Perhaps there are several reasons the headmistress wants her off school grounds... 'Oka... y.'

'Oh! Another thing. We're in the middle of school exams, so I'll be leaving all the marking for you!' (This was something else Janice despised with a passion.) 'I'm here until the end of the week but, who knows, I might leave earlier now you're here. I mean, there's nothing like being thrown in the deep end, is there? Ha ha!'

Emma forced a smile at Janice's evil laugh. That's not even close to the truth. She thought. You're launching me overboard into the ocean and leaving me to drown!

The shrill triple-beeping of the bell rang out around the school, enticing the children into action. Chair legs scraped across the floor as kids jumped into the aisles. Literally.

Emma watched, amazed by their release of pent-up energy. They bounced up and down, turning, smiling, and clapping, excited to be escaping from the classroom. The chance to run, shout, and scream in the brisk September air was tantamount to ecstasy.

'Great!' Janice clapped her hands together for some form of conformance and sighed when the jumping and smiling continued. 'Okay, everyone outside! Remember You have got a Maths exam after the break.'

Her remark stopped the kids' excitement in seconds and groans echoed around the classroom.

'Miss, I didn't have time to study because my gran hurt her leg and my mum…'

'I don't want to know, Michael. You've got all break-time to study.'

'I forgot to take my book home.'

'Not my problem.'

'I've lost my book.'

'My dog weed on mine, and I think it's still on the washing line.'

'Out, get out, all of you!' Janice wafted them towards the door. 'Go to the playground and study, study, study.'

Emma watched them file out, shoulders slumped at the news. She vowed not to dampen their spirits when she was in charge.

***

At the close of Emma's first school day as a teacher, her energy levels were bordering on empty. She couldn't remember when she'd felt so exhausted. Who'd have thought a class of six-year-olds could zap my energy so quickly? She thought. Emma soon realised she needed to be in a constant state of alert. Vigilance was needed every single second of the day. The phrase: "having eyes in the back of your head" had never sounded so poignant.

When the children left the classroom, running like the school was on fire, Emma returned the flat shoes to Janice.

'Thank you very much.'

'It's no big deal. Thank YOU very much. You are giving me my ticket out of here!'

'Won't you miss it?'

The long pause before Janice replied became uncomfortable for them both.

'Yes, and no. I'll miss the regular payments, for sure!' Emma didn't know what to say.

'Don't look so shocked,' Janice said. 'Look, some people do it as a vocation and others do it for the money. Unfortunately, I'm in the latter category. Not that they pay a fortune, mind you, but at least it's regular money. And it's a job.' She picked up her handbag and slung it over her shoulder. 'See ya tomorrow!'

Emma watched her stroll out of the class and wondered if Janice's forthright approach was part of the reason she had been asked to leave.

Despite Emma's bad beginning, she had enjoyed the day. The time had flown quicker than she had imagined possible. She was looking forward to teaching these young minds and getting to know them as individuals. But right now, she wanted to leave.

Her attention turned back to the footwear problem. She tried several times to stick the tape back around her ankle, then gave up.

'Oh, the hell with it!' she said and limped out of the classroom, and down the corridor. As she weaved her way across the playground towards the car, she wore one shoe and carried the other. Like a warrior with a weapon, she was poised and ready to bludgeon the first person who made any sort of detrimental comment.

Once in the safety of her car, she grabbed her phone and rang Sue, her best friend.

'Hi! How did it go?' Sue's perpetual cheerfulness radiated down the phone.

'Horrible. I need a drink. Can you meet me at the wine bar?'

'Yeah, sure. Half an hour?'

'Perfect.' *That gives me time to treat myself to some new shoes before going for a drink.* Emma removed her other shoe, then drove away in bare feet, hoping not to be stopped by the police. That would just about make the perfect end to an awful first day.

By the time Sue arrived, Emma was already on her second glass of white wine. She'd wolfed down some crisps, and the empty packet lay on the tabletop, folded in a perfect, tiny triangle. It reminded her of Chris. He'd shown her how to do it.

Sue plonked herself on the comfy seat next to her friend, flicked back her long black hair, picked up the crisp packet, and grinned. 'What's this? A visual aid for tomorrow's maths class?'

Emma giggled. The effects of the wine had lightened her mood. 'No, stupid!' She took the offending triangle, threw it under the table and stamped on it, imagining it was Chris' head.

'Careful there, girl. It's just a crisp packet. It looks like you're trying to kill it.'

Emma wasn't in the mood to explain its symbolic significance, so she flicked it under her chair where she could no longer see it.   'So, come on,' Sue said. 'Tell me all about it. I bet you could eat all those cute little faces.'

'I don't know about eating. Beating might be a better word. Some of them are little monsters. I must have the only job in the world where you can say: "We don't lick the pencil sharpener", and it almost seems normal!'

Sue burst into laughter, and Emma filled her in on the rest of her stressful first day.

'What a disaster!' Sue's statement resonated around the almost empty establishment. 'Are you gonna go back?'

'Of course, I am! I've given up my old job for this, haven't I? I don't have a choice. The money's better, obviously, but boy do you have to work for it!'

'Ugh! Don't talk about money to me,' Sue sighed. 'I'm back living at my parents' house; can't get a job and I'm living off their handouts. It's so embarrassing.'

'Sorry,' Emma said. 'But, if you study a hotel management degree and won't relocate to a tourist area, you are limiting yourself, don't you think?'

'Yeah, yeah, I know. You've got a point!' Sue gave a weak grin. 'So, what about the other staff members?' she said, changing the subject. 'Are there any hunky guys?' She wiggled in her seat with anticipation.   'No. Most of them went out with the ark. They're your typical middle-aged teachers. You know the type. The men all wear tweed jackets with elbow pads.'

'Urgh!'

'The main colour for males and females seems to be beige.'

'Lovely!' Sue's sarcasm wasn't lost on her friend.

'You know why they all wear elbow pads, don't you?'

Emma shook her head.

Sue put her elbows on the table and placed her head in her hands. 'Oh no, not this again!'

'Silly cow!' Emma laughed.

Sue always brightened her mood, whatever the situation.

*

About the author:

Biography

In a past life... okay, when she was younger, Michele was a dancer, magician and fire-eater, who toured the world for over twenty years in theatre, musicals and circus.

During her years in entertainment, she also worked as a contortionist and a knife thrower's assistant. She assisted a midget in his balancing act, appeared in a Scorpions concert and has been in the Guinness Book of Records for being part of the world's largest human mobile. She has rubbed shoulders with Sting, Chris de Burgh, David Copperfield, Claudia Schiffer, Errol Brown and Maurice Gibb from the Bee Gees.

When she retired from entertainment, she went back to school, gained a First-Class Honours degree in Modern languages: English and Spanish and studied for a Master's degree in Education. As well as writing, she owns and runs her own English Language school in Spain.

As a writer, she has won several awards and competitions for her work, which has appeared in annuals, anthologies, magazines and national newspapers.

She lives with her Spanish husband, Randy, a dog, a cat and two terrapins. Michele loves living in the countryside with views of the sea and likes nothing better than to sit on the terrace at the end of the day, look up at the stars and contemplate.

Books by Michele:

Fishnets in the Far East: A Dancer's Diary in Korea (A True Story).
https://books2read.com/u/mqwpWe

Fishnets and Fire-eating: A Dancer's True Story in Japan.
https://mybook.to/FishnetsJapan

Fishnets and Fleeting Contracts (a true story). Coming out in 2024.

Ravens' Retreat (A paranormal horror story).
https://mybook.to/RavensRetreat

The Circus Affair. (A romance with a touch of crime).
http://mybook.to/circusaffair

Say Yes to Everything. (A comical Christmas romance) Coming out November 2023

An Education for Emma. (Romantic comedy). Coming out in December 2024

The Forest of Forgotten Time (A haunting story of evil) Coming out in January 2024

Summer Season at Sandy Coves Book 1: Kitchen Thefts and the Vengeance Club. Coming out in February 2024.

Summer Season at Sandy Coves Book 2: Murder at the Manor. Coming out in March 2024.

Summer Season at Sandy Coves Book 3: Hubble Bubble, Poison Trouble. Coming out in April 2024.

Look out for other titles by this author!

Michele can be contacted/followed at:

https://www.facebook.com/michele.e.northwoodauthor

Twitter: @northwood_e

https://www.pinterest.es/nextchapterpub/pinterest-board-michele-e-northwood/fishnets-in-the-far-east-a-dancer-s-diary-in-korea/

If you would like to be informed of future releases, giveaways, competitions and free books, send me an email to michelenorthwood@gmail.com

Printed in Great Britain
by Amazon